Lives of the Fathers

ILLINOIS SHORT FICTION

A list of books in the series appears at the end of this volume.

Steven Schwartz

Lives of the Fathers

UNIVERSITY OF ILLINOIS PRESS
Urbana and Chicago

Publication of this work was supported in part by grants from the Illinois Arts Council, a state agency, and the National Endowment for the Arts.

This book is printed on acid-free paper.

"Lives of the Fathers," *Ploughshares,* May 1990

"Return with Us Now to Those Thrilling Days," *San Francisco Chronicle* and *The Village Advocate,* Fall 1985; winner of a PEN/Syndicated Fiction Award

"Uncle Isaac," *Missouri Review,* Fall 1989

"Q12081011," *Mid-American Review,* Spring/Summer 1990

"Summer of Love," *Puerto del Sol,* Winter 1991

"Navajo Cafe" first appeared in *To Leningrad in Winter* (Columbia: University of Missouri Press, 1985)

"Down Under," *Virginia Quarterly Review,* Summer 1985

"Other Lives," *The Literary Review,* Winter 1990

"Legacy," *Antioch Review,* Fall 1988

"Madagascar," *Chicago Tribune,* September 1988; winner of the 1988 Nelson Algren Award for Short Fiction

Library of Congress Cataloging-in-Publication Data

Schwartz, Steven, 1950–
    Lives of the Fathers / Steven Schwartz.
        p. cm. — (Illinois short fiction)
    Contents: Lives of the Fathers — Return with us now to those thrilling days — Uncle Isaac — Q12081011 — Summer of love — Navajo cafe — Down under — Other lives — Legacy — Madagascar.
    ISBN 0-252-01815-X (cl. : acid-free paper)
    I. Title. II. Series.
PS3569.C5676L5 1991
813'.54—dc20   90-27908
                                                                      CIP

For Emily

Contents

Lives of the Fathers

My father is telling me about Victoria again. I smile, nod, remind him I am a journalist and that I cannot just sit down and write a book about Victoria because he is sure it will make a bestseller, full of romance, intrigue, and heartbreak.

"It's rags to riches to rags again!" my father says, not listening. "A story you won't be able to put down!"

"You've told me."

"What happened to her would be no big deal today but back then, who did such things? She was a bohemian! And beautiful, everyone says so. It's a tragedy! And don't forget the love story here, Adam. The composer. At that time he was nobody. That anybody should know he would become Mr. Hollywood, least of all Victoria! The two of them were bohemians! In Atlantic City they'd take a room together at the Shelburne—torn down years ago—and go to the shows and the dances and the burlesque houses, and the liquor they drank . . . all without care what people thought! They believed in free love. Okay, so maybe it's not front-page news now—"

"Please, Dad," I say. "Can we get on with this?"

I am helping my father move into an apartment outside Philadelphia, a few miles from the house he has lived in for thirty-seven years. My mother died last year and although he didn't want to move, the place has become much too big for him. "I forget things. I'll come home from shopping and leave the groceries in the car and then I'll look out the window later and see the trunk open and remember that's where the groceries are and I haven't finished taking them in." He told me this over the phone, long distance to Tucson, where I work for *The Arizona Daily Star.* "Maybe if I had a smaller place I could keep track of things better." It was the opening I'd been waiting for. "I'll help you move," I said. After our mother died, my sister and I had begged him to find a place he could manage; he wouldn't consider it at the time. "Where will you find a view like this?" he said, pointing to the park across the street.

But in thirty-seven years—the house is as old as I am, my parents moving in two weeks before I was born—the area has deteriorated. Next door, on what used to be the spacious front yard of an older home, three small bungalows have been squeezed together, only eight feet apart, the minimum allowed by code. And the park, neglected over the years, has litter clinging to the backstop of the baseball diamond where I once charged around the bases and dove head first into home, winding up in the hospital with a broken collarbone (I was safe). The once stately oak trees at the park's entrance stand like weary, bent petitioners at a gate, too many unpruned branches broken and dead from storms, swinging loose in the wind like discarded canes. On weekends and holidays teenagers wash and wax their cars on the grass, letting the soapy water run into our driveway. My father sees none of this, just his preserved view of many years ago: my sister and I on skis about to descend the mild incline of the park's snowy hill toward a stream that now has soft drink cups and hubcaps floating in it.

"A beautiful woman once, even your mother admitted as much. Gorgeous red hair and a figure that made history. Like a goddess she walked around. Yet innocent. She knew nothing. A schoolteacher she wanted to be when I met her. No wonder he fell for her."

"Who?" I say. My father has a habit of referring to everyone as "he" or "she," a problem worsened by age.

"The composer," he says, looking at me surprised. "He was nobody back then, a few minor songs he wrote. Victoria showed them to me. Believe me, my own were better."

Today the composer is a famous man, an Oscar winner for his movie themes. This is the "love interest" my father wants me to include. My father sees it all, the innocent girl from Philadelphia, the New York composer (unknown and struggling at the time) falling in love on the boardwalk, Victoria's subsequent initiation into decadent Manhattan society, their torrid ten-year affair, the terrible fights, his jilting her after she is hooked on drugs, her acting career ending in nude photos for girlie magazines, the simultaneous meteoric rise of the composer ("True to life," my father says, "the S.O.B. gets what he's after!"), the eventual end of Victoria in an institution, where she leads a reclusive life for the next twenty years.

"I'm telling you," my father says. "It's what the public wants to read. You can't take an hour a day to work on an idea that will bring you millions?"

I wrap the wine glasses in newspaper and put them in the box. My father is holding up a decanter that I remember us using only once—the night my parents had an engagement dinner for my sister and her husband, who live in Seattle now. Before my mother died, my parents bickered constantly. Whatever anger was buried during our childhood surfaced in those later years after my sister and I moved away from home. My father, insisting my mother not work (she'd been an office manager in a Manhattan bookkeeping firm), had taken her away from her five sisters in New York to Philadelphia, where he wanted to settle after the war. Her lifelong struggle with agoraphobia grew worse here and frustrated them both. Near the end she was afraid to leave the house at all for fear of . . . well, anything from crime to not having a bathroom nearby for her bladder which was always acting up from her diabetes and the drugs she took for high blood pressure. My father retired to take care of her (he wouldn't put her in a nursing home), helping her to the bathroom, getting her meals, doing all the shopping, making the beds, keeping the house clean. My mother didn't want a maid. The house had been her whole life. One minute she would yell at my father for overworking himself, the next she would complain he didn't do things right: the way she'd

done them when she'd been able to get around. Nearly blind
and barely able to walk, she nevertheless followed after him,
criticizing him for the way he loaded the dishwasher, wiped
down a table, threw in the laundry without sorting it first, left
the butter out, put away silverware . . . "Who ever heard of
keeping silverware in a second drawer?" she'd say. Or "You
bought that lousy Tyson's chicken again." Or "Why didn't you
get that Tyson's chicken we always eat?" My sister and I pleaded
with my father to just bring someone in; what was Mom going
to do? Stop the person from cleaning? He wasn't young himself,
seventy-two. But he wouldn't hear of it. "She'll pull out of this,"
he'd say, blind to my mother's condition, desperate to deny
anything was really wrong. "She's just venting," he'd say. "It
doesn't bother me. She puts up with my craziness and I put up
with hers. We've been doing it for forty years. That's what love
is." And he'd go back to buying the wrong kind of mayonnaise
or running the dryer on high or ironing a blouse that she hated
to wear, a thousand little stubbornnesses they assaulted each
other with every day. I think it would have gone on like this
forever had she not suffered a stroke and been helpless to protest,
paralyzed, unable to raise even a finger to scold him. He brought
in a housekeeper then, a victory for neither of them.

Now, my first time home since the funeral, my father and I
haven't spoken once about my mother's death, how frightening
and horrible it was to watch her decline. Instead, he talks only
about Victoria. "I never touched her, Adam. She would call and
say, 'Newman, I'm lonely. Why don't you ever come see me?
I'm by myself here tonight.'"

"So why didn't you go?"

"Go? To see her? I was a married man by then!"

"But before that, when she was the bohemian on the boardwalk or whatever—didn't you even date her?" I can't believe I've
gotten suckered into this discussion.

"Of course I dated her—but I never touched her! 'What a
gentleman you are, Newman,' she would tell me. 'I've never met
such a nice man,' she'd say. I gave her music lessons, every
Thursday at four. I taught her the piano, boogie-woogie. She

wanted to be a jazz singer for a while. I brought her home to meet my mother and father and brothers! Did they like her?"

I shrug. "Did they?"

"Of course they liked her! Everyone did! She was a beauty! Hair down to there." My father motions somewhere with his hand, the basement—or hell. I don't know. I'm losing track of the day and the conversation. In a week I have to be back at work, and Marti, my wife, is seven months pregnant with our first child. It's not a time I particularly want to leave her alone.

"Dad, can we talk about Victoria tomorrow? We should concentrate on packing. You just let me know what you want to keep here."

"I'm telling you, this is an idea you can count on a hundred percent. You make a little outline and send it off. I guarantee you'll get fifty offers."

"It doesn't work like that. So let's forget about the book—"

"A blockbuster! We're talking wide audience appeal. The younger people will understand the bohemian side, the rebellion. Him—"

"Who?"

"Her father. He was a stiffened Prussian who could spit cold water on you, icicles. You see what I'm talking about here? She rebelled against him. He was this main influence on her life and she ran away from her family to be with him—"

"*Who?*"

"The composer! That's the part the kids can relate to. I've got notes to show you."

"No, please. I don't need to see them. I can imagine it if I ever want to write about this."

"So you'll do it?"

"Let me sleep on it, Dad," I say, just to calm him down.

"He saw her naked."

"What are you talking about?"

"Fred Rose. The photographer. He took pictures of her for her portfolio. She wanted to be an art model then. I saw them one day on his desk when he was out to lunch, the big envelope with her name. I couldn't look."

"That's considerate of you," I say.

"Did I tell you she'd have hold of my arm as we walked down the aisle of the Robin Hood Dell to our concert seats? I don't exaggerate, thirty heads would turn."

"Why didn't you marry her?"

"Him," he says.

I throw up my hands. "*Who,* Dad? Can't you use names?"

"I'm sorry. The composer. She fell in love with him while we were going out. One day I went over there to take her out to Fairmount Park and there was a note on the door: she had to see me that day—urgent. I called her all day, all evening, late into the night. I couldn't close my eyes without being frightened what had happened to her. The next day I call and she tells me she thinks we shouldn't see each other anymore. She's going to marry this young songwriter."

"The composer."

"Right. But at the time, I'm also writing songs, so I feel doubly bad. Not only has she thrown me over for another guy, but he's a songwriter too."

"So then you met Mom."

"Many years later. I was a different man then. In my thirties."

"You carried a torch for Victoria all that time?"

"Sure, what's ten years when you know someone like her?"

I shrug. My father says, "Tomorrow we'll go see her. I haven't spoken to her in twenty-five years but I think I'm ready now. You'll go with me and take pen and paper, right? It's all settled."

"No, Dad," I say. "Ab-so-lute-ly not."

Victoria, Bohemian of the Boardwalk.

This is the title my father wants me to use for the novel about Victoria's life. We are driving down Route 95, on our way to Wilmington, Delaware, where Victoria lives in a nursing home.

"Dad, you don't just drop in on someone you haven't seen for twenty-five years."

"Why not?" he says. "Won't she be surprised."

Victoria's brother, who owns an appliance store in South Philadelphia, has given us the address. Early this morning my father

called him and said we wanted to visit Victoria. I was writing
a book about Victoria's life. I heard all this as I was coming
down the stairs, with sleep in my eyes, my mouth dry, aware
that we'd hardly accomplished anything together yesterday. All
night I'd been up packing while my father slept on the couch.
"Just going to take a little five-minute snooze," he said, and he
was out for the rest of the evening.

We pull up in front of the Golden Meadows Care Center. In
the lobby several people in wheelchairs and bathrobes are watching television. There is a chalkboard with a list of such activities
as Senior Aerobics, Health Awareness Check, and Creative Cake
Decorating.

Someone calls to my father. "Mr. Holzman, how you doing?"

It is Moses Rudolf. I haven't seen him in over fifteen years.

"Moses," my father says, "I had no idea you were here." Moses
is in a wheelchair, one of his legs gone. He sees us staring down.

"Blood clots," he says. "Been quite a while now. How you all
doing?" He extends his palm flat out for us to shake hands. I
look down at his black hand with the same amazement I did
as a child. Moses had worked for my father in the jewelry store
in Philadelphia. When my father would go out to lunch, I'd stay
behind with Moses and watch the store. Look here, he'd say,
and show me how all his fingers could bend back at the knuckles.
His elbow reversed too, so he could stroke the long skull of his
head with his fingers as if it were another person's hand. It was
both exciting and repelling, especially since he'd put opal rings
from the showcase on his fingers to do it.

I take Moses' hand in mine and shake it. His hand is warm
and I can almost feel the opal rings pressing into my palm. His
hair, which used to be tight black curls, lending him a sinuous
invincibility, now is thin and white, and I can see the pinkish
brown skin underneath. It occurs to me that he is at least ten
years younger than my father, who, with his blue knit golf shirt
and arms tan from working in the garden, looks like a picture
of youth next to Moses.

"So what you all doing here?" Moses says. "I guess you all
didn't come by just to see me—or my better half." We laugh

nervously. "It been a while," Moses says. "I'm used to it by now." I try to picture Moses—the double-jointed arms and elbows of his one-legged torso—bent back and stroking his head preciously. It is a frightening yet enthralling image of roving, serpentine arms, like a Hindu god, and has the same power to make me stare dumbly at him as I did years ago.

"You retired youself, am I right?" Moses says to my father.

"Ten years now," my father says. "I was ready to leave." He spreads his hands out, as if to contemplate a globe while he speaks. "Comes a stage when you have to consider making changes. Life's too short to spend so much time in one place."

"Here today, gone today," Moses says. "How's the wife doing?"

"She's dead, a year now."

"Sorry to hear that. I didn't know nothing about it."

"To be honest, it was a blessing for her. Very sick. Great pain for her."

Nobody says anything for a few moments. Then Moses asks, "How about you, Adam? What you doing now?"

"He's doing terrific," my father says before I can answer. "A big reporter out in Arizona." My father bends over and taps Moses on the shoulder with a stiff finger, speaking in a stage whisper. "He broke that Mafia story on the Nicosi family in Tucson. You read about it, right?"

Moses shakes his head. "I just keep up with the sports."

"We're going to have a baby," I say, trying to add something I care about. The Nicosi family turned out to be nothing in the end, dismissed at the grand jury level for lack of evidence. My father forgets to add this, as he does anything that might diminish my greatness in others' eyes. When I was in law school he liked to tell everyone I had an internship lined up as a law clerk at the Supreme Court. "I only *inquired* about one," I told him the summer after I dropped out.

"Well, congratulations to you, Adam. You gonna make a fine daddy."

"Yes?" I say, and wonder about this, why his casual compliment strikes me with such force, and then I realize it's because my father has never said anything so simple and easy to me. "Thanks," I say softly.

"He's writing a terrific book about her."

I wince. Moses looks puzzled.

"We're here for someone named Victoria," I explain.

"Schmidt," my father adds. "You know her, Moses?"

Moses shakes his head. "Can't say I do." A bell rings. "Lunch time. You all want to join me?"

"We should find her, Dad," I say. "Ask at the desk about her."

"Moses," my father says, "I know where you are now."

"You know where I am," Moses says. "Don't be no stranger."

"You can see the woman she used to be, right? I mean, for the book you could use your imagination, now that you met her."

I don't say anything. I'm driving back. It was obvious once we left the nursing home, with his shortness of breath and hands trembling as he searched himself for his keys, that he'd been too shaken by the experience to drive. Near the Pennsylvania state line, we have traveled almost twenty miles from the Golden Meadows Care Center in uncomfortable silence. But the farther we drive from the nursing home, from the real Victoria, the more I can feel my father regaining his confidence.

"You should hear her laugh. She wasn't up to it today. De-lightful. Like a little arpeggio." My father raises an imaginary flute to his mouth and plays fanciful, silly tones that sound as if he's inhaled helium. "I used to live for that laugh. Once—"

"Stop it, Dad."

I pull off at a rest stop.

"You have to go? Go ahead. Do your business. I'll wait here."

"Listen to me," I say. I turn off the engine. He squirms in his seat.

"All right, maybe it wasn't such a good idea. I warned you she might not be in such good shape."

"Good shape? She was pitiful."

"Tragic, I told you, it's a tragedy what happened—"

"It's not a tragedy, it's just pitiful. Did you look at her? Did you?"

My father doesn't answer. I think of Victoria, sitting on a plastic chair in a corner of the recreation room, her mouth and throat scarred by cancer, her hands clutched at her stomach as if to hold a warm stone there, her complete lack of response to my father's pleading *It's Newman, Victoria, it's Newman,* his hand on her bony shoulder, the dull green fabric of her robe with its Save the Whales button that an attendant had pinned to a worn lapel.

"We'll go visit her again while you're here. She may need time to feel comfortable with seeing me again."

I shake my head. "Who exactly are we talking about? Victoria?"

"Sure, Victoria."

"And you can't see how hopeless she is? She didn't even know you were there!"

My father gets out of the car. He goes over to a picnic table and sits down with his hands on his knees. There's a row of newly planted spruce trees behind him, staked down with wires. On a blanket in front of the trees a family sits eating lunch. A toddler industriously picks up paper cups and drops them in a cooler, takes them out and drops them in again. I feel a pang of loneliness for Marti, for our unborn child, my own family. It seems months since I've been gone.

"I've always been an optimist," my father says.

"Listen to me. You can't just throw this fantasy into the pot and make everyone come out happy."

He doesn't respond.

A truck pulls into the parking space in front of us, the whoosh of air brakes being released.

"Mother's dead. You never mention it. You never admit it. I can't get around that. I can't even help you move out until you acknowledge that in your heart—grieve over it for God's sake! It's got you completely stuck, and me too now."

We are sitting beside one another like two old men on a park bench, with all the time in the world. Not a word from him.

"You don't face things," I say, driven now to force a reaction. "You won't even visit her grave with me."

He remains mute. When I turn I see that his eyes are moist and my heart seizes. He pats my knee. "We won't talk about her anymore," he says, leaving the pronoun eternally ambiguous.

That night my mother sits with me in a sewing room on the third floor, a floor that doesn't exist in my parents' house. A plaid blanket lies over her paralyzed legs, the same blanket my father covers himself with, summer or winter, when he sleeps on the couch.

Why won't you come down? I ask her. She has been up here a long time.

How is the baby? she says. There's no strain in her voice, none of the tension I remember as a child when she would tell my sister and me to go to our rooms and play because she was sick and needed to lie down.

I let her know the baby is fine, Marti too. Will you come down now? Please?

She pulls my father's blanket tighter around her waist.

We need you. *He* needs you.

My mother lowers her head and parts her hair with her fingers, exposing the white roots. I look closely and discover a tiny gem, like the red dot Indian wives put on their foreheads, only this jewel is deep blue. I wonder how long it has been there, how it is embedded in the skin.

Does it hurt? I ask.

My mother smiles at me. I will be disappointed when I wake up, because she hasn't looked at me with such pleasure and curiosity in a long time. No, she says, it doesn't hurt.

Does Dad know about this?

She laughs. All the fathers know, she says.

A week passes. I'm still in Philadelphia trying to get my father moved.

"He's impossible," I complain to Marti during one of our late-night phone calls. My father is asleep on the couch as usual.

It is where he used to sleep when my mother was sick. He has never dropped the habit.

He has been to see Victoria every day since our first trip. His visits grow longer, stretching out to three, four, and five hours. He tells me he is "making progress," though I have no idea what this means because I refuse to go with him, staying behind instead to pack, angry at him for leaving me with this task. My editor has reluctantly given me another week's extension, and Marti has become impatient, listening in cool silence.

"Maybe you're part of the problem," Marti says now.

"How do you mean?"

"He can rely on you to take care of everything while he goes off and lives out this fantasy."

"What can I do? I have to get him out of here. The realtor is calling every day asking whether we'll be out by the closing."

"Will you?"

"I don't know. We'd better. It's three hundred dollars a day if we don't."

Silence.

"What's wrong?" I say.

"I just miss you, Adam. This was supposed to be our last vacation before the baby."

"If I could just get him away from Victoria."

"It wouldn't matter. He'll find some other way to keep you there. He's afraid. He doesn't want to be alone."

"How are you doing?" I say, wanting to change the subject. "Still being drop-kicked?"

"Every night right at ten, just as I fall asleep. Apparently baby doesn't want to be alone, either."

"All right," I say, "I get the message. I'll try to wrap things up here in a day or two."

But the next afternoon my father returns from the nursing home and informs me that he's bringing Victoria to dinner tomorrow evening. He'd like my help in preparing the meal. I'm stunned.

"In the car," he says, explaining how he'll transport her here. Shouldn't it be obvious?

"Dad, are you actually talking with her now?"

"Of course I talk with her."

"Does she talk back?"

My father looks at me as if I'm crazy. "What do you think— I go around talking to myself?"

"I can't believe it. I just can't believe this!" I've been staring at the dining room table pads for the past half-hour, wondering which of my three piles they belong in: the apartment pile, the storage pile, the trash pile. Unable to decide, I put the pads in an "undecided" pile, which grows exponentially as we near our deadline. We have three days left before the new owners take possession. I called my sister in Seattle to ask for help, but her vacation starts tomorrow and the whole family is leaving for Hawaii. "Why didn't you call earlier?" she asked.

I thought I could do it myself. I wanted to. She had spent so much time here when our mother had a stroke; I felt this was my contribution. "Have a moving company do it," my sister said last night. "They'll put everything in boxes and get it on the truck." But it's too late for that now and I would feel even more ashamed of my failure to accomplish this task. Also I've gotten sidetracked by mulling over my own past, high school yearbooks, honor roll certificates, desperate letters to adolescent girlfriends whose faces in memory blur into a composite not unlike the youthful, fiery Victoria laughing in the salted sea air of the boardwalk.

"You need to help me pack, Dad. I'm sorry, but you're going to have to postpone the dinner."

"I can't," he says. "It's our anniversary."

"Your anniversary? Of *what?*"

"When we first became engaged."

"You were engaged now!"

"For a day. Then she called it off. She'd gone back to her home in Darby, run away from the composer. She called me, crying. She said he was all wrong for her—no respect, no security, no future. Later I learned he'd taken up with somebody else and that's what she was so upset about, but at the time all I heard was she wanted to marry me. She begged me. I had all the stability the composer couldn't give her, a pretty good business over on Samson Street. It was right after the war and I was selling diamonds like postage stamps. I couldn't keep enough in stock—"

"Wait a second. After the war—you were already with Mom, weren't you?"

My father stands at the refrigerator, eating what's left of the rice pudding. He keeps his back to me. "We were engaged, too."

"Too! You were engaged to Mom *and* Victoria at the same time?"

"Yes. That same day Victoria called me I gave her a ring."

"Mother knew about this?"

My father nods. He puts the lid back on the rice pudding and pushes it far back onto the shelf filled with the leftover takeout food we've been eating every night. He refuses to look at me, won't move from behind the refrigerator door.

"In other words, you broke off the engagement with Mother."

"It was a bad thing. Very serious."

"I'll say."

"She shouldn't have taken me back."

"Mother?"

"She shouldn't have taken me back. Or she should have forgiven me. To be married all those years and never forgiven. She's also to blame." He closes the refrigerator. Rice pudding has stuck to his chin. I reflexively touch my own face, so much the image of his, reversed only in that it shows shock, where his shows resignation. "You look back and you say, I should have done things differently. But you look back hard enough and you know you wouldn't." He shakes his head. "You wouldn't. It's a whole new life you need. I'm going to nap."

"Dad—"

His eyes close on the couch. In seconds he's asleep.

*   *   *

"More wine?" my father says to Victoria.

We are sitting at the dining room table, surrounded by boxes stacked up to the ceiling.

Victoria raises one finger. My father smiles and fills her glass to the rim with the wine, a white Bordeaux.

She wears a blue dress with a silver satin collar, a small white bow fastened with a cloth button the size of a kitten's nose to each short sleeve, the elastic of which fails to grip her upper arm. A hairdresser who visits the nursing home every Thursday has coifed Victoria's white hair, swept back and folded behind her head with what seems a generous amount of hair spray. At her throat rests a pearl choker—my father's gift to her for their "anniversary." We have gone through appetizers (breaded broccoli and zucchini from Mateo's), and veal (from the Chalet), and now on to dessert, a Black Forest cake (from Engleton's). My father spent the entire day gathering food from the best restaurants in town. He unpacked a set of dishes and some silverware from one of the boxes I had sealed. He pretended to be making all the food himself in the kitchen. As far as I know, Victoria believed him.

"Adam, would you do the honors?"

My father sets the cake in front of me with a knife. "Excuse me," he says. Victoria leans over to say something to him. She cannot raise her voice above a whisper, the throat cancer. "Victoria says none for her." She whispers again. "She wants to know why you didn't eat your veal."

"It's inhumane," I say.

"I slaved for hours," he says.

I smile weakly at him, then glance at Victoria, her eyes glassy from the wine, her thoughts only half here as she stares off toward the ceiling while my father takes her hand and helps her up from the table. She has moved in and out of being with us during dinner, speaking only twice, with great pain, once to say the food was excellent, the other time to inform us that at eleven she would be picked up by her mother (who died twenty years ago). The staff at the nursing home made a big production about her going out. "She had four attendants dressing her!" my father announced over dinner, his arm paw-like, hung like a large gourd over her tiny shoulder, squeezing wide-eyed looks from her as she sat mute and dazed in all her aged smallness. "It could have been her first dance! You should have seen everybody standing on the steps waving goodbye. Do you know she hasn't left the grounds there for fifteen years? It's a miracle she's here."

Earlier we had stood in the kitchen "preparing" the meal, a hush-hush operation while Victoria sat in another room waiting for the end of an imaginary toast, her arm extended for the five minutes we'd been gone, a courteous if strained smile on her face. Meanwhile my father and I had had a tug of war over the dinner plates, with him insisting he would wash and repack them and me demanding he use paper ones.

Now my father sits with Victoria in the living room while I clean up. I hear him talking to her although I cannot make out what he is saying. It sounds as if they are having an actual conversation, punctuated by laughter and teasing. I dump all the Styrofoam containers and paper cups into the trash, then wash the silverware and repack it. The movers will be here tomorrow and I am finally ready for them, having marked every box with the appropriate apartment room. The sense of accomplishment I feel from all this is ridiculously great.

When I enter the living room, I see my father sitting at the feet of Victoria, who, between the wings of a floral chair, has only her legs visible to me in their navy hose. I picture Victoria's face, imagine her pale yellow eyes staring vacantly at my father, a dimly lit warmth retrieved from near hopeless depths.

"Victoria will be staying for breakfast," he says.

She leans forward. Her expression conveys shyness and mild flirtation. The bows on her sleeves dance with mischief, her pearl choker a high marble wall to be surmounted for the pleasure of her throat, her exhausted body all things to all men. I do not see the hollow flesh, the dead cells, the bones so fragile they break like tiny glass tubes, the laying her out sacrificially on my mother's bed.

I run upstairs and lock myself in his bedroom. I call Marti.

"*He wants to sleep with her*," I hiss into the phone.

"Adam? Is that you? Where are you?"

I cannot believe how my heart has begun palpitating. "I can't allow this."

"Victoria and your father?"

"Yes," I say. "*Yes*. It's crazy. He's crazy. He wants me to witness all this, make me an accomplice, prove to the world he's finally captured her. This ultimate expression of his megalomania!" I motion downstairs, as if Marti can see me. "He can't do this. It's against the law."

"He's forcing her?"

"Against the law of *nature*."

"Where are you now?"

"Upstairs. I've locked the bedroom door." From below I hear my father calling me.

"Adam, you can't stop them."

"Marti, this is my father we're talking about. He's about to defile this poor woman. For God's sake, she's been in a nursing home for twenty years! She doesn't even know what's happening to her! She can't take care of herself. It's cruelty."

"Does he love her?"

"What's *that* have to do with it?"

"Does he?"

"Marti, the question is utterly inappropriate here."

"Is it?"

Neither of us speaks for a while. I play with the switch at the base of the nightstand lamp, an antique, the one item I've left unpacked because I want to take it back with me. I consider knocking the whole thing over, the delirious sound the brass shade will make. Marti says, "All right then, are you coming home tomorrow like you promised?"

"Do you realize the situation that's developed here tonight? I can't just let him destroy her like this. He has no compunction, no awareness of what he's doing. It will *kill* her."

"Adam . . ."

"What?"

"I want you back."

I put the phone against my shoulder. Downstairs I hear music. The piano. A snappy tune marches up the stairs, twirls and descends.

"I want to know something," Marti says. A high C pings over and over, like a knife tapping crystal. A music lesson? "Are you going to be the same kind of father?"

"I don't understand."

"Never around. Never here for your child."

"Of course not," I say, but a shiver goes through my body.

"Because if you are . . ." Marti starts to cry. "Because if you are, I want to know about it now. I *have* to know."

I think about Marti's parents, divorced after thirty years, her mother saying to us on a visit from California, "I was Sleeping Beauty—in reverse. He kissed me and I fell asleep for thirty years."

"We're going to be fine," I say.

"Don't tell me that. It's not true. And you can't promise me anyway. You're not even here now."

"I didn't have a choice, Marti."

"Why did you wait until I was too pregnant to fly before you went? Were you trying to get away from us? Is it that you're scared of being a father?"

"Marti, look," I say, but I'm not sure what I want her to see. That I've pleased no one by coming here? That my father married the wrong woman? That my mother died trying to find love in this house? That my father, demonic in his obsession, is about to fuck the lights out of the dead, rotting past?

"I'll be home tomorrow. I promise."

"But do you *want* to come home?"

"Are you kidding?"

"I want to hear you say it, Adam."

"I want to come home. I want to see you. I love you."

"You love our baby?"

"I'm crazy about our baby."

"How do I *know*? Can't you tell me something that will make me believe you?"

I'm lost.

"Adam?"

"I'm yours," I say, simple enough. "That's what love is." I shake my head, unable to believe I'm quoting my father. "I'm yours."

I sit for a moment after I get off the phone. Under the green felt bottom of the brass lamp I've placed a photograph for safe-keeping. I pick up the picture and study it: my mother kneeling beside me, her arms wrapped around me. Her eyes are dark brown—clear of illness. The side of her face is crushed against mine; she hangs on with a passion to have me unfairly in her arms forever. I am six years old and missing my front teeth, toothlessly ecstatic to be in her embrace, so that now, looking at the child pulled toward her in desperate love, I feel the lock on my heart break, and silently I cry out for her.

When I go downstairs I see my father at the piano playing a song I know from childhood, the words about a young man who pulls the moon along on a string so the tide will rush out and he can dance at the bottom of the sea with his lover. On the couch, with her arms at her sides, is Victoria, and for a moment I think she is dead. My father gets up from the bench and goes over to her. His lips touch her ravaged cheek, caress the back of her neck, move up to the bony protrusion at the base of her skull. I see the brainstem quiver with life under their warmth. He strokes her hair, then looks up at me and tells me with his eyes to mourn us all.

Return with Us Now to Those Thrilling Days

Lately, Daniel has been locking himself in his office with the lights off, afraid to answer the door, then leaving after six, when he is sure no one will see him. He has not told his wife, Jean, about this, nor that he has started seeing a counselor who assures him his anxiety and depression are more common than he might think, especially for men around his age. Daniel and Jean both teach at the community college, Daniel in history and Jean in art. They travel often (no children), attend neighborhood block meetings, participate in Educators for Social Responsibility, play volleyball in the parks program, and work Saturdays for two hours in the community garden. They live in Eugene, Oregon, a town with "high livability" where they both can imagine growing old.

Tonight is Daniel's thirty-fifth birthday and he is having a Sixties party to celebrate. He is hoping that by returning in time he will discover what is keeping him from moving ahead. Arnie and Lisa, the only guests to arrive so far, are sitting at the table with him, while Jean is finishing the food she has been preparing all day. She brings out two large jugs of wine marked NOT GALLO (Daniel has pasted on the labels, remembering the boycott) and a mock apple pie made from Ritz crackers. "I always wanted to bake one of these," she says, "and now that I did, it tastes just as awful as it looks. I remember doing acid one night and staring at the picture on the box, thinking, Real or unreal? Mocked or unmocked? God or unGod?"

Lisa laughs nervously. Daniel can tell the conversation is making her uncomfortable. Nineteen years old, she looks more Esprit new wave than Sixties radical—silk headband, Porsche sunglasses, glow-in-the-dark necklace, and toy hand grenade on a purple belt. Arnie wears an old army jacket with his last name written in magic marker across the pocket. Arnie's divorce was finalized three months ago and for a while, in a panic, he rushed around dating anyone with whom the slightest bat of an eyelash had been exchanged. Then he met Lisa, a student intern in his ad agency. Daniel knows Arnie is going through the same thing as himself but has found a solution, a temporary one at least, in a young girlfriend.

Someone knocks loudly at the door. "A fateful rapping," says Jean. "It's open."

In steps Coogan, huge, woolly, dressed in a Nehru jacket.

"Where'd his neck go?" Arnie says.

Coogan lifts one finger for quiet. He takes a medallion from his jacket pocket, hanging the gold-plated disc around his neck.

"Oh, flashback!" Jean says.

"Your pants could match better," Arnie points out. They are Scotch plaid with two-inch cuffs. Despite being six-foot-five, with a black and silver pirate's beard that makes him look fearsome, Coogan is a gentle farmer, a committed pacifist—happy in his solitary and rustic life. He takes an art class from Jean at the college. Twice a week he drives in from the country, where he lives along the McKenzie River and raises vegetables so big they could walk on legs in cartoons. Insisting such growth is natural, he never uses chemicals or anything more than beer in cups to catch the Northwest slugs that eat his lettuce. He's been to Findhorn and has seen what is possible with love and meditation, he tells everyone.

Daniel checks his watch. "Nine o'clock."

"Relax," Jean reminds him. "No one's going to be punctual."

"Maybe we shouldn't have had a theme party."

"Oh, cut this out, will you?" Jean says. "People will be here."

"A lot of my friends have negative feelings about the Sixties," Lisa says. "Most of them think it was a failure."

Nobody says anything.

Coogan pulls a button on his Nehru jacket. "I heard two girls talking on campus last week. One of them was asking the other, 'South Vietnam, was that the communist one?'"

"You know," Daniel says, addressing his comments to Lisa, "you shouldn't think of the Sixties as a movement—I mean people didn't enroll in the Sixties any more than they did in the Depression of the Thirties . . . or the nuclear terror of today. It was just a time is all, not a club you joined."

"I know that. Only my friends—"

"Well, tell your friends to read a little, educate themselves."

"Hey," Jean says, "be nice."

"Yeah, and don't be so hopeful," Arnie adds, trying to both make a joke and console Lisa, who has been hurt more by the tone than the substance of the remarks. Daniel stands up. "I'm sorry," he tells Lisa, knowing he is only making his outburst worse by walking out of the room—but also knowing he has to leave immediately.

He goes into the bathroom, where he stands over the sink and runs the water. He takes a deep breath, then another, then splashes cold water on his face. When he tries to look in the mirror he sees once again that he has forgotten to turn on the light, the darkness becoming a habit with him now when he is alone. The party should only last five or six hours, hardly anything compared to his thirty-five years. Yet even minutes seem unbearable trapped in the house as a host. Why did he do this? It suddenly feels ridiculous and pretentious, the arrogant scolding he gave Arnie's girlfriend, the invitations he sent out quoting everything from the *Bhagavad Gita* to Tiny Tim. He wishes the big surprises of his life were still ahead of him instead of behind: knowing what he will do for a living . . . *if* he can make a living; catching himself noticing young girls with more affection than lust—and being more relieved than alarmed; discovering he can cope with unbearable loss—a daughter nine months after she was born: pneumonia, coma, then nothing, except a decision not to have another child, a decision that surprised them both, since it wasn't from fear or remorse but from loss of wanting. He tells himself he'll recover from this, also—this strange mixture of malaise and dread that has lasted too long to be a mood.

More guests have arrived when Daniel comes out. People are no longer clustered around the kitchen table but have spread to the living room, sitting crosslegged on pillows.

"Put your tape on," Jean says, smiling at him supportively. She is wonderful, truly generous, Daniel thinks. He must snap out of this for her.

Two of their friends from volleyball have just come in, tie-dyed from headband to socks. Everyone claps. Daniel puts on his tape, four hours of oldies beginning with "Great Balls of Fire" and ending with "The Long and Winding Road"—a project that has absorbed him for weeks. He had expected to be at "In a Gadda Da Vida" at this point. He gets the bottles of NOT GALLO and brings them to the center of the room, serving people. More guests come, a rush of feathers, beads, leather, stones, shells, silver, and fringe. Someone shouts to look out the front window. A tractor pulls up and from it steps a couple in overalls, Daniel's department chairman and his wife, in bright flannel shirts, one carrying a washboard and jug, the other a paper bag full of plastic kazoos, which are distributed to everyone. Next to Daniel stands someone breathing hard in a gas mask. "Great party, pal," he says.

An hour later, a group of people have settled into the bedroom where the heavy smoking is going on. Coogan is there, too, although he does not smoke grass anymore or even drink. He is telling them how he got out of the draft.

"Divine revelation," he says, pausing to polish his medallion with the cuff of his sleeve. "I smuggled a plastic baggy of vanilla soda into my Jockey shorts. When it came time for the urine sample, I poured the vanilla soda in the cup instead. I figured they'd let me out for diabetes. But when I strolled over to the nurse's station I suddenly remembered being told they could keep you overnight and test you again in the morning. I was sunk. There I was, holding my cup of vanilla soda, handing it to the nurse as my urine sample, realizing my scheme wouldn't work. The nurse looked at me and said, 'That's the darkest specimen I've ever seen.' And it suddenly occurred to me—total clarity, one shot of the arrow, the perfect Zen response. 'You're right,' I told her, 'I'd better run that through again.' And I did, took it back and drank it all down. I got my 4-F immediately." Coogan breathes on his medallion. "There are some things more horrifying to the army than killing," he says, "even if they are an illusion."

In the study, Jean is consoling Mary Ann about Arnie. Mary Ann has forced herself to come to the party. She's determined not to arrange her life according to where or when Arnie might turn up. But what she didn't expect was to be so paralyzed by the sight of Arnie sharing a Turkish pillow with his new girlfriend.

"You were together ten years," Jean tells her. "Even if you accept it intellectually . . . which you do, don't you?"

Mary Ann nods.

"You still need time to feel it in your bones."

"I hate being reduced to pudding," Mary Ann says. "Why am I hiding in here like this?" She stands up. "I'm thirty-six years old, with a career of my own. I'm not afraid of loneliness. I can handle solitude. My days are completely full without as much stress, and I don't even have to pretend I enjoy my privacy. I honestly do. Does this outfit look all right?" Mary Ann has come in black pants and a rose-colored blouse. Her socks are the only daring part of her appearance, one blue and one orange. She never felt comfortable dressing for the Sixties, and the socks are the best she can do toward letting go.

"I want to tell you something," Jean says. "You're one of the most beautiful women I know."

Mary Ann laughs over this, but Jean can see the tension disappear immediately from her face.

"Maximum effort, minimum attachment," Coogan says, when asked his secret for growing giant vegetables.

"Tell your draft story again," someone says.

Daniel is dancing with Lisa, a slow song ("What Becomes of the Broken Hearted"). They do a long, elegant, silent, soft dip at the song's finish, touching fingertips. He is relaxed for the first time this evening, enjoying dancing with her, so much more clear and satisfying than talking. This is the best way to apologize to her—to anyone, man or woman, touch fingertips and dance in feathery grace. But when the song is over, Arnie drops his Panama hat on Lisa's head, breaking the spell. Ownership, Daniel thinks, a Sixties issue.

"We have to change our whole way of thinking," Coogan says. "It has nothing to do with logic or negotiations. We're caught up in duality—inside, outside, mine, yours, win, lose. *Of course* they're the enemy. *Of course* we're afraid of annihilation. We'll always be afraid as long as we see the situation in terms of us against them—to be part of one you have to fear the other."

"Is this a we're-all-one rap, Coogan?"

"Think about it. What's the solution? Less bombs? More bombs? A joint command center? A better hot line? Nuclear parity? Whatever that means. A freeze? A Republican? A Democrat? A Socialist? A survivalist? Do you really think it has anything to do with options? It's not a crossword puzzle. Not the solution to Rubik's cube. It's simply . . . ."

Coogan drops his medallion dramatically on the floor. He'd seen Alan Watts do this once at a lecture: finish his sentence by dropping a glass of water on the table. Although stirred, Coogan didn't know what it meant then, either.

Coming out of the bathroom, Jean bumps into a man with a gas mask. "Great costume," she says, being friendly. He passes her an empty roach clip. While she is staring at it, he moves his hand across her breast so quickly she is unsure if the touch is intentional. But when he nods his head toward outside, she has no doubts.

       *   *   *

"Make a wish, birthday boy," the man in the gas mask says. Daniel is down on his knees, blowing out the candles, thirty-five of them. What he wishes is that something enlightening will happen this year, something decisive, something to build on. "Blow out the candles, Daniel," says Jean. What is he waiting for? The man in the gas mask gives Daniel a nudge in the ribs with his knee. Daniel blows them out. He waits for them to come back on. Jean did that to him last year. But the candles go out completely, smoking. This is it. No tricks. Thirty-five.

"Everyone feels inadequate," Arnie is explaining to Lisa. They have gone to the backyard and are lying in the hammock together. Arnie is trying to reassure her that she is not inferior to his friends inside. "You shouldn't compare yourself to anyone," he says, "because it will inhibit you, take away your spontaneity. Show people what you have inside you, not what you think they want to see."

"I don't know what's inside me," Lisa says. He always tells her not to worry about what people think, but she winds up trying to do this as just another way to please him, another rule to obey, one more expectation from somebody. She's afraid to tell him that she has never done anything completely for herself. Where does she begin? Falling in love with Arnie was something she did on her own; no one expected her to be interested in a man twenty years older, just divorced. And if she's never herself, why does he like her? Does he see something in her she doesn't yet see in herself? Some potential? She always feels he knows more about her than she does about herself, has some answers she doesn't even yet have questions for. She can still hear Daniel's words: Educate yourself. I've got a 4.0 average, she wanted to say, I get A's in everything, always have . . . but now realizes how foolish this sounds, how it's exactly what he was talking about: she doesn't know anything except school and how to take notes and repeat what other people tell her.

"What's that?" Arnie says, hearing what sounds like a scream.

After Daniel finishes cutting the cake, Jean takes him aside to tell him about the man in the gas mask, his quick feel.

"I knew there was something weird about that guy," Daniel says, and walks over to him.

"Excuse me, would you mind telling me who invited you?"

The man in the gas mask looks down at Daniel. He is tall, almost as big as Coogan, but without the weight. His eyes seem to become tiny through the transparent panes.

"Friends of the owner."

"I'm the owner. Which friends invited you?"

"Your friends."

The man's movements are clumsy, uneasy, slightly drugged it appears. His hair is greasy and long, out of place even for this party. When he tries to stand up straight to challenge Daniel, his back remains bowed.

"This is a private party," Daniel says. "I'd appreciate it if you'd leave." He likes the way he is handling this, steady and careful, not threatening but firm.

The man leans against the wall with his arms folded. "I was invited."

"If you won't leave, I'll have to call the police." Daniel starts toward the study. The man in the gas mask follows him in, then quickly closes and locks the door.

Jean screams when Daniel says the man has a knife. Don't do anything.

They have been in the room for thirty minutes. The man in the gas mask sits in the recliner, adjusting its height with the lever on the side, looking through a photography book on national parks. Daniel sits on the floor by the phone. The knife lies open on the arm of the recliner. It has a white plastic handle with a silver emblem and looks like the switchblades Daniel remembers seeing for sale in Nogales, Mexico. Daniel has been trying to reason with him. The man insists he has been invited by friends, although he refuses to point them out or even name them. He's absorbed in the book, looking at the pictures through his gas mask, breathing through the air holes, occasionally stopping to turn the book sideways as though he were examining a foldout.

"Why don't you take off your mask? You must be hot."

The man looks up. His eyes narrow and become wary. Even though his collar is buttoned at top, part of his neck can still be seen, discolored and badly burned.

"Come on, take off the mask," Daniel coaxes. "What are you afraid of?"

The man covers the plastic panes with his fingers and sobs behind the mask.

Jean is nearly hysterical. She keeps calling in and checking on Daniel, only to have him assure her he's all right and not to do anything drastic. The party is divided on whether to call the police. Coogan is leading the faction that says to be patient. Arnie, Mary Ann, and Lisa want to call immediately. The three of them have become allies during the crisis and temporarily forgotten about their history.

Coogan says the police will only complicate the situation. He can tell from Daniel's voice that he means what he says about not doing anything.

"What else can he say?" Mary Ann shakes her head in exasperation. "The guy is holding a knife on him."

"Give him a chance," says Coogan. Then he has an idea. He motions for people to follow him to the door of the study. Everyone has been squeezed into the kitchen, whispering. He begins to sing.

"Oh, no," Mary Ann says. "I cannot believe this." Coogan is singing "Give Peace a Chance" through the door. He gestures for people to join in. Some do, reluctantly, with rusty voices. Lisa whispers to Arnie, not without some irony, "Is this what the Sixties were like?"

"You don't have to be embarrassed," Daniel says. "Just walk out of here with me. I don't know what the problem is, but you can stop things from getting worse by leaving quietly." Daniel is surprised by how boldly he speaks; the variables are all good for confidence—a knife, not a gun, a sobbing rather than violent loony who may not be harmless but doesn't exactly seem dangerous either. Perhaps the only reason he took out the knife was because he felt cornered. The way to get him to leave is to reassure him, while taking control, Daniel has decided. "I'm going to stand up. If you want to follow me, that's fine. If you want to wait in here until I've asked everyone to leave the party first and then come out, that's fine, too. Whatever you want. Your decision." Daniel stands. The man clutches his knife. His whole body seems to shake. "This is a lousy party," he says. "I expected more." Outside the door it sounds like drunken singing—hearty, tuneless, growing in volume.

Jean dials the emergency number. The police operator asks if anyone is armed. "Yes," Jean says, *"yes,"* and starts to cry because she remembers how Daniel told her he would never protect himself in fights as a child.

Daniel walks out first. He motions everyone aside. Following him is the man in the gas mask, who looks neither left nor right. Daniel heads for the refrigerator, where he takes out a six-pack and hands it to his former captor. Then they go out on the porch and stand together talking. Daniel shakes hands with the man and then watches him disappear into the dark. People burst out from inside (they've been pressed against the front window) and surround Daniel, cheering for him, Jean hugging him, everyone trying to touch him.

In the distance they hear a helicopter coming closer. It circles overhead, shining its spotlight on the house. Through a bull-horn, the police identify themselves. The spotlight sweeps across the lawn and stops on Daniel, who has gone to the edge of the grass to communicate with the hovering machine.

"We're all right!" he says through cupped hands. "A private matter, we took care of it." The helicopter continues to hover above them. People are drunkenly waving, blowing their kazoos.

Daniel cups his hands again. "NOT TO WORRY!" he shouts up. The aircraft seems to understand this, whirring away quickly into the night.

*   *   *

There is something about the relationship of memory to action that he does not understand. Something obscure and deceptive, historic and mythic, something that turns the present inside out and makes it a living past—something he can't articulate to the guests who crowd around him hungry for details. He must settle for explaining the facts: the knife on the chair, the crying, the moment of "truth" when he stood up. But what really happened Daniel doesn't know, only that the experience is starting to elude him, motion becoming a memory.

At his car, Arnie kisses Lisa. The events have aroused them both and they can hardly wait until they will be home. But when Arnie tries to drive away, the right front tire thumps. "Jesus," he says, "a flat. A goddamn flat." Lisa puts her hand on his shoulder, but his desire is waning, the momentary thrill gone.

Mary Ann sees the flat even before she nears her car. Dennis, a friend from work, has walked her up the dark street. "Why me?" she says, but suddenly realizes she has just as often asked the opposite (why not me?) and that these two questions have relentlessly snapped at her ego all her life like two mad hounds. She is tired of them, sick of their senseless howling, set off as much by a flat tire as a divorce.

Dennis bends down to inspect the tire. He runs his hand along the wall. "It's been slashed," he says.

For good luck and to quiet the insatiable hounds, she whistles "I'm a Little Teapot," and lets her hand drop on Dennis's knee.

In the back of Coogan's Volkswagen van is a mattress. Several of the guests, who are too stoned or drunk to drive home, climb in and fall on the bed. Drunk as they are, they do not fail to notice the thump thump thump of the ride, a noise that beats at their temples like a balled-up sock. They yell at Coogan that it sounds like a flat. "No problem," he says. "It will heal itself," and he keeps driving.

*   *   *

Daniel has been helping people change tires all morning. Some of the guests blame him for the damage, not having anyone else around to fault. They say he let the man in the gas mask escape, only to slash their tires. Daniel doesn't answer. He keeps taking off lug nuts. He knows better than to argue with irrational guests. He has offered to reimburse them, and Jean has made several pots of coffee. But the guests still feel betrayed and foolish, since earlier they'd been cheering him. When he finally finishes, it is close to 5 A.M.

In the bathroom, Jean brushes her teeth and thinks that the party will be considered a success despite its unfortunate ending. There will be a ton of litter to clean up in the morning, beer cans, dirty dishes, globs of dip, cigarette ashes, and all the lost items: sunglasses, earrings, necklaces, beads, lighters. The other subject she thinks about is her marriage. She wonders what can save it, whether Daniel's brooding will continue, whether they will come out of this decline as they have others. She doesn't believe Daniel thinks seriously about their marriage anymore. He is in love with some great, unformed idea—some promise of transformation. Jean wonders why she has never had these illusions, whether it has something to do with being female, why she is satisfied with the slower, more steady progress of her life, why she cares and worries so much about him, but knows she will be the one to finally say "Enough." And leave.

Daniel sits in the living room waiting for the sun to rise. He is too excited to sleep. He has gotten hold of something tonight. He must be careful not to overlook its significance. It was only a moment and it may be gone in the morning, but he was released—dazzled by its brilliance. He sits on the couch, his hands squeezed tight, his mind burning with the intensity, trying to recapture all of it.

Uncle Isaac

My Uncle Isaac's sexuality, according to my father's theory, had been marked by the half-woman. Isaac, at thirteen, would sneak into the basement of the Philadelphia Medical Museum, where a woman's torso floated in formaldehyde. It was 1933, and here—beneath the museum's upper floors with their public exhibits—research and training about venereal disease was taking place. In a reinforced glass case, at the back of a laboratory room filled with charts and diagrams of progressive syphilis, rested the half-woman, clean of infection except for a lesion on her left breast.

Isaac would stand transfixed in front of her, unable to turn away until the danger of discovery became greater than his fascination with the blue-white breasts preserved in their fluid, their otherwise perfect shape and appearance marred only by this blemish. I felt sorry for my uncle when I heard this story. I don't know what he thought about on those visits. Who had she been? Would she have loved him? Could he have saved her? Would she have let him touch her? When my father told me the story of the half-woman, as a way, I think, to explain something to himself about Uncle Isaac, I was fifteen and I already knew sex could drive a person crazy with curiosity. And in 1933, without access to any books or magazines or even textbooks, perhaps the half-woman was Uncle Isaac's only recourse. This, though, I think was my explanation for what I found incomprehensible, too. Isaac, eventually caught by one of the doctors, was punished by his father, forbidden to leave the house for weeks, beaten and told he had a filthy mind. "Our father should never have done that," my father told me. "Then maybe none of this would have happened."

My father felt protective toward his younger brother. Isaac had weak lungs and had almost died of pneumonia at an early age. And, too, he could not talk well with people. My father, on the other hand, blue-eyed and tall, gregarious and warm, was popular with the customers—Isaac and he were partners in a furniture store. They were supposed to be equal partners, but it was my father who made all the major decisions. Isaac did little in the way of selling, coming out from behind the cashier's window only if it was absolutely necessary, whereas my father would do anything to make a sale: put his hand over his heart, sigh, cluck, moan, appear to pray, purse his lips, shield his eyes, smack his forehead, fan himself, raise his hands to God, and even make his eyes moist—all in the service of selling a Barcalounger.

Isaac, meanwhile, took care of the books.

There was a period when I was about eight years old that Uncle Isaac began seeing a woman who worked next door at the bank. A redhead, she would meet him right outside the store and they'd go off to lunch together every afternoon. He would say goodbye to her outside, too, and never introduced her to my father. One day she wasn't there, they had broken off, and shortly thereafter the woman moved out of town. For two weeks Uncle Isaac didn't come into work and then when he did there was something slow about the way he moved, as if he'd been ill. My father and mother talked about him in their bedroom at night and although I tried, I could only make out whispers. I asked my father during this time why Uncle Isaac had never married and an uncomfortable look came over his face, one that I would later understand meant he was giving me an answer he thought best, though not necessarily true. "Some people are just happier alone," he said. Unsatisfied, I went to Isaac himself. "Why didn't you marry the redheaded lady?"

"She went away, Andrew."

"Why?"

"She wanted to live in another town."

"Why?"

Uncle Isaac smiled at me. "Here," he said. "Why don't you play with this a while?" He sat me down in a chair at a desk and brought over an old adding machine. He said I could push the buttons and pull the long handle to watch the numbers appear in red on the white tape. I did this for a little bit, then became bored and asked him again. "Did you love her?"

Uncle Isaac stapled a payment card to a folder.

"Did she love you?"

"I think you should stop this now, Andrew. You're making me angry." It was the first time Uncle Isaac had ever become cross with me and I slumped down in my chair, hurt. After this incident he became less friendly, until he acted toward me as he did toward everyone else.

When I was thirteen, my father had a warehouse sale that he put me in charge of running. I was thrilled by the respon-sibility, the trust he placed in me. The warehouse was around the corner from the store, and I loved being near all the activity and the men who worked there. Pete was the warehouse su-pervisor, and Leroy and Farcourt were the truck drivers. Pete was always shouting, but in a good-natured way. "Where's the invoice for McDermit! What the hell's going on with this console—it's supposed to have legs! Who stole my pen!" Leroy was tall and never raised his voice. Softball was his first love, and the only time I'd ever seen him say no to my father was about working overtime when he had a softball game. "No, sir, Mr. Sapperstein, I got to pitch." You could barely hear Leroy when he spoke—his voice started somewhere behind your head and came into your ear like a wisp of smoke. Farcourt, on the other hand, looked and talked like Little Richard and never stopped his flow of sexual self-approval. "Who is pretty? Not me. Who the boss? Not me. Who got the brains? Not me. Who got the power of the hour in his love trumpet? That me." He would take me aside and say, "Who you be making cry this

week, Andrew? You got you a little Sally to be *oh! oh!* so good
to you? What is love, my friend, except the boxing of two hearts
in the ring of desire?"

I smiled at Farcourt and continued putting price tags on the
furniture. During the sale, I was to wait at the door for customers and then ask if I could help them find anything. Most
people would just want to browse, my father had told me. We
had mainly tables and occasional chairs, bureaus and smaller
chests, a few complete bedroom or dinette sets, but mostly there
were odd pieces from discontinued lines. We had some relics,
too, brass umbrella stands with mermaids etched on the sides,
alligator-skin luggage, baby strollers with large black hoods, all
items my father once sold before the store specialized in furniture. While my father was overseas during World War II, Isaac
had taken over and almost gone bankrupt. A bank loan needed
to be renegotiated by my father when he returned. He eventually
pulled the store out of the red, and then told Isaac to stick to
handling the back office, one more resentment Isaac must have
held against my father, one more time my father's competence
highlighted Isaac's failure. All this is speculation, of course,
because it has been more than twenty years since we've heard
from Isaac, and I've wondered if his actions toward me were a
way of expressing his bitterness at my father, the good brother.

At 10 A.M. we opened the doors of the warehouse and people
came in who had been waiting outside. Any fantasies I had
about imitating my father's salesmanship quickly vanished. We
could barely keep up with the questions.

Where's the other piece that goes with this whatchamacallit?

Can I buy that one by itself?

Why's this leg wobbly?

You have this in another color?

Who's in charge here—you?

I was kept running the whole morning and into the afternoon,
taking money and answering questions, repeating again and
again, "As is, as is; no, that's all there is." Farcourt was on a
delivery and Pete was in his office tracking down two lost ship-
ments from High Point, North Carolina. That left Leroy and

me to rush around taking money and making sure people didn't tear into the boxed merchandise that wasn't for sale. At the end of five hours only some magazine racks and one chest of drawers were left. We decided to close and count the money—almost three thousand dollars. I hadn't expected nearly that much and was about to walk the money over to my father when my mother came by to pick me up for an orthodontist appointment. Since we were already late for the appointment, I asked Leroy to take the money around the corner to the store.

When my father came home from work that evening, he sat down on the couch next to me and said, "Andrew, was there a problem today at the sale?"

"What do you mean?" I'd been eagerly awaiting the moment all night—when he would come home and proudly congratulate me on the money I'd made for the store. I had thought (in my fantasies) he might even call first, surprised and whooping with delight, and I'd pestered my mother throughout the evening about why she thought Dad hadn't phoned.

"Pete told me most of the stock was cleared out."

"It was," I said. "Leroy and I sold everything but a few pieces."

"And you put the prices on I told you?"

"Yes."

My father looked at me for what seemed an unbearable moment. I could tell he was trying to choose his words carefully. "Do you have any idea where all the money might be, then?"

"Leroy had it. Three thousand dollars. Didn't he bring it to the store?"

"He brought the money to the store, but there was less than three thousand."

"It wasn't three thousand exactly. It was two thousand nine hundred ninety-three dollars. And thirty-six cents."

"Well, what I saw was quite a bit less than that."

"How much less?"

"Two hundred dollars."

"Two hundred dollars less?"

"No, that was the total amount."

"What!" I felt panicked. I was sure I'd counted correctly—not that huge of an error at least. "What happened after Leroy brought the money over?"

"Isaac put it in the safe and then I made a deposit on the way home."

"Maybe Isaac counted it wrong, or left some of the money out. I don't know. We made that much, Dad. I counted it twice."

"Well, we'll straighten it out in the morning. I'm sure there's an obvious explanation."

But the next day, a Saturday, I couldn't think about anything except the money. As soon as I woke up I asked my mother if Dad had called. "No, Andrew," she said, a little firmly. "Are you going to ask me this all day?"

So I called him myself. The secretary told me he was busy with a customer; he would call me right back. I waited by the phone, unable to go across the street to the empty lot and play football. A game was starting up, one usually did on Saturday morning, but I was tied to the phone. Finally, it rang.

"Andrew? Louise said you called."

"Well?" I said.

"Well what?"

"Did you talk to Leroy?"

"It's his day off."

"But can't you call him? Can't you just call him at home and ask him how much money there was? I don't think you believe me." I felt completely misunderstood, singled out for something I hadn't even done. "You're not taking this seriously," I said. "It matters to me that you find out what happened. It's a lot of money!"

"I know it's a lot of money," my father said. "And, yes, I am taking it seriously, too. Just give me a few minutes to get things organized here."

He promised to call me back within the hour, but the hour passed and then another and finally I begged my mother to call him. "He's your father, Andrew," she said. "It's all right for you to call him."

But he'd suddenly become much more (or much less) than my father, I wasn't sure. A lawyer, my accuser, someone to whom I could never prove my innocence. I had all sorts of crazy thoughts that just got worse the more I tried to push them out of my head. Leroy was telling him he saw me stuff hundreds into my pockets, my pants bulging with the money. Or Farcourt had persuaded Leroy to split up the money and make me the fall guy. I was sitting outside on the porch, waiting for the phone to ring, and I covered my head with my hands and shouted Stop this! Stop this! when my mother called out the window that my father was on the phone. I hadn't even heard it ring, so loud was the noise in my head.

"Andrew," my father said, his voice calm as usual. "Leroy confirms your story."

I didn't like his use of the word "confirms"—it sounded so cold and, well, legal, but I was deeply relieved, then guilty again, this time because I had been suspicious of Leroy, and even Farcourt, who hadn't been there.

"Dad," I said, "that only leaves Isaac. Have you questioned him yet?" It had to be Isaac.

"Take it easy, Andrew," my father said. "No need to accuse anybody of this. Especially your uncle."

"But Dad—"

"We'll take it over from here, Andrew. Is your mother nearby?"

I handed the phone to my mother. I was astonished they could go right into talking about the dinner party they were having this evening. When my mother got off, she said, "Why don't you go out and play for a while, Andrew?" as if I were still a child.

I rode to the store on my bike, a long ride but I had to speak with my father and make him understand the urgency of this matter. He was talking with a manufacturer's representative. I stood to the side, out of the way, and listened to my father say they wanted to double the shipment on twin beds and to make sure the order was here before Thanksgiving. The salesman from the factory nodded, wrote the information down. "You're doing terrific out of this location," he said, flattering my father. But it was true, business was taking off.

"Well, hello," my father said, surprised. "Did Mom bring you here?"

I shook my head. "Can I talk to you a minute, Dad?"

"Sure," he said. I was amazed I'd caught him at a free moment. "Let's go inside the office."

Behind the office's glass window I could see Isaac bending over the huge NCR, slipping yellow account records to be tabulated into the metal tray.

"I know it's him, Dad," I said without any introduction.

"Andrew . . ." His voice had tightened one more notch from this morning. "I want this to stop—now. It's a very serious thing to accuse someone as you're doing."

"I know it's a serious thing, but it's a serious thing to lose three thousand dollars. I made all that money for us! I don't want anybody to think I took it!"

"Nobody thinks that. We're trying to solve the problem. But you don't go around pointing fingers at people until you have evidence. We have certain rights in this country."

"How do you know he didn't take it? He was the only one to touch the money after Leroy, right? Who else could it be? The money is in his apartment somewhere. I bet if you searched there you'd find it!"

My father told me to lower my voice. He pulled his chair closer to mine and spoke softly. "I'm going to put your bike in the car and take you back home. You're much too upset about all this."

On the way home, he told me Isaac would have no reason to steal the money. As a partner in the business, he could take an advance of up to five thousand dollars anytime he wanted—with my father's approval, of course. Something my father never needed from Isaac.

Weeks passed and nothing happened. My father brought in the police, but since the money was "undocumented"—that is, only Leroy and I knew the actual amount and there weren't any receipts—nothing could be proved. So they were going to let it drop.

My grades started to slip, especially in math, where I couldn't concentrate on word problems, ones with sums of money in them. At the mention of dollars or cents, my mind would zoom off, and I'd be tapping my pencil and clenching my teeth—once even mumbling aloud, "I know he took it." When my teacher asked what was wrong, I shrugged, the same thing I did at the lunch table when my friends asked why I had quit the tennis team. Every day instead I hid outside my Uncle Isaac's apartment to observe. What did I expect to see? Bookies jotting down numbers? Mafioso pulling up in Cadillacs? I saw only the same third-floor, dark corner apartment, with its curtains closed, and then the light going on when Isaac came home and stayed in every night.

I questioned Leroy over and over again. He was polite and kind and promised not to mention that I'd asked him. Always his answer was the same, his story consistent. He had brought the money by right after I left. He'd pushed it through the cashier's window to Isaac. That was the last he saw of it. Why didn't you get a receipt? I asked him.

He looked at me. A receipt? What for? What I'm gonna need a receipt for from the Sappersteins? He spoke about the Sappersteins as if I weren't one of them.

I talked to Farcourt. Had he noticed anything funny? He had been at the store when Leroy came by with the money, having just finished a delivery.

"No, baby, I didn't take your money."

He knew what I was saying, how crazed with suspicion I'd become. Whenever I came to the store now, I watched everyone. I'd stand at the door, inspecting every interaction, every transaction that went on, a grim child of fourteen. (I'd had an uneventful birthday during all this and, yes, true to myself, had wished for the money to be found.)

I even watched my father. Not out of suspicion but with the hope he would do something. At least make Isaac take a lie detector test. No, he would not subject his brother to such treatment, especially to a test whose accuracy was questionable anyway. To me it sounded as if my father had decided to take Isaac's word over mine, my honor sacrificed so he would not have to face what his younger brother had done. The incident remained a troubling mystery, my father admitted, but there was nothing more he could do.

Listless at school, tired from not sleeping well, unable to concentrate and dozing in class, I would laugh a few seconds too late at a joke, look away while someone was talking, stare at my lunch and then decide I wasn't hungry. One morning I couldn't get out of bed; my body was paralyzed, the right side. I could move my left arm, my left leg, but everything on the right side had stopped, that side of my face included.

I was taken to the hospital, given a neurological exam, blood tests, an EKG, spinal examinations, a whole battery of tests that took two days and turned up nothing. A psychiatrist was called in to see me and I told him I didn't know what was wrong. He asked questions about girls and about sex. Was there any problem at home? Was I afraid of anything? No, I said. Yes, I liked girls. No, I hadn't had sex but, of course, wanted to, and no, nothing was different about home.

Then the right side of my face quivered, a spasm. "There's some money missing. . . . " I told him the whole story—how no one believed me and it was driving me crazy. I'd tried to forget about it but I couldn't, I just couldn't.

"What would help?" the psychiatrist asked me.

"Uncle Isaac," I said. "If they at least questioned him." That night when my father came to visit, he told me he had thoroughly questioned Uncle Isaac, who said he'd received only two hundred dollars. "I know it's him," I said. "I just know it." My parents looked at each other. They were worried and frightened for me. "Could I question him?" I asked. "Just let me ask him?"

So they agreed to bring Isaac in. My voice came out strange, from half my mouth, twisted and distorted, but finally I had my chance and Isaac stood at the foot of the bed. He was wearing a blue jacket and carrying an umbrella. He looked concerned about me, which was upsetting because I wanted him to look guilty, afraid. I asked him about everything he remembered, from the time Leroy handed him the money to the moment he gave my father the cash to make a deposit. He had counted the money shortly after Leroy brought it over. Where was it in the meantime? Locked in the cash drawer. Did he see anyone go near the drawer? No, he was the only one in the office at the time. What happened after he took the money out? He counted the bills, then included the amount in the nightly deposit which was put in the safe. Did he see all the twenties? The fifty-dollar bill? The two hundreds? (I remembered the railroad worker who had just been paid and gave me two hundred-dollar bills for a big carpet.) No, Uncle Isaac said, he didn't remember bills of large denominations, only ones, fives, tens, and a couple of twenties. Did he tell my father how much we'd made? No. Why not? The amount wasn't significant enough to mention. "It was, it *was!*" I cried out. An ugly sound, wounded and helpless, came out of the half of my mouth that could talk. My parents hurried in from outside the room where they were waiting. He's getting upset, my mother said to Isaac. You'd better leave now. Uncle Isaac said he hoped that I would be well soon. He'd shaved the mustache he'd had for years, the flesh above his lip naked now and milky smooth, the cloudy color of old ice. There was a roundness to his features, different from the withdrawn, sharper features of Isaac in the office. Here he had almost all the fullness of the moon in his face. All this softness looked and made me sad, ashamed that I had caused everyone such trouble.

I nodded my head and thanked him for coming.

After a week, physical therapy started for me. First just my fingers, then my whole hand—I was told to visualize my fingers grabbing my tennis racket or gripping a spoon of ice cream, familiar, comfortable images. Soon, I was able to stand up on my right leg, holding onto the wall and then, after some time, I'd recovered almost all my mobility. No physical cause was ever found and I went back to school after four months.

I had to work hard to catch up—and I did. Worked fiercely, spending extra time in the language lab, French being my weakest subject. To my friends, who knew only that I'd been struck by a mysterious illness and who had sent cards and come to see me in the hospital, I was a hero who through determination had become well. Once again, I made jokes and talked about sports and about girls. I tried out for the tennis team and made it, a better player now than I'd been before. Our coach said I had the guts to win and held me up as an example of what willpower could do. I quietly accepted the praise, the attention, the success of winning games with heated volleys, while my mother, and even my father, taking time off from work, both of them loving me all the more for my recovery, came to watch me receive the trophy for our team after we took the regional championship. I had won eleven straight matches in the boys' singles, taking the last two sets of the final competition 6-1, 6-0. Each time I hit the ball it was with a solid fury, low and centered, my knees springy but not too loose, a brilliant rage sweeping the racket swift like a sickle across my body.

It was one night just before summer began. I had started going out with my first girlfriend and we'd lain down together in the woods behind her house. Her skin smelled sweet, and when I moved my head further down there was the deeper, harder scent of her breasts and she let me unbutton her blouse. She did not push my head away but wound her fingers through my hair, with a strength that surprised me. We twisted around one another, each change in position tighter and quicker to lock us together than the last. No clothes were taken off. Nothing "happened," but I remember it as being the first experience in my life of unyielding lust. I came home and lay in bed and thought that sex was the most powerful force I'd ever known—the sensations wouldn't let go. I wanted to think of nothing again, nothing besides this feeling.

Around midnight the doorbell rang. I heard my mother and father both get up and my mother say, "See who it is first," and then my father's heavy footsteps down the stairs. The next voice I heard was Uncle Isaac's.

My mother put on her robe and went downstairs. In a few seconds she cried out, Oh God! and then Isaac said, No, please, don't. I sat at the top of the stairs listening. Their voices carried

up and I tried to hear above the pounding of my heart. Uncle
Isaac was telling my father he wouldn't be coming in to work
anymore, that he was going away. His voice, strained and excited, sounded unnatural.

Where? my father asked.

He didn't want to say. He was just going away for a while.
There were some things he had brought with him, some account
books my father needed to know about. My parents said nothing. Their silence was eerie, for neither of them was likely to
be quiet at a moment like this. I couldn't imagine what they
were thinking.

Why didn't you tell us? my father said. Why couldn't you let
me know? Didn't you think I'd want to help you?

Isaac didn't answer. I tried to picture what they were doing.
Were they just sitting there staring at one another?

Everything is written out, Isaac finally said. All the records
numbered with explanatory notations. Anyone with a decent
bookkeeping background will be able to pick up from here.

My God, my father said, and then again, my God, my God.

Apologize to Andrew for me, Uncle Isaac said.

There was a long pause and then I heard my father speak
carefully: What do you mean?

I took the money.

I ran downstairs, my heart racing; I was gulping air. I'd been
freed, vindicated. Uncle Isaac was sitting on the love seat with
his back to me. When he turned around I saw his face, the long
lashes and powdered white skin, the jet-black wig, the red lips
as if soaked in cherry juice, the stained teeth, the half-smile of
triumph.

Q12081011

Mr. Chester told David he would not pass tenth grade unless he passed gymnastics. "You can do it, boy," he said. "Just tuck your head under and let the momentum carry you."

David shook his head. "I can't."

"Can do," Mr. Chester said. "Repeat after me. Can do."

"Can do."

"*Can do,*" Mr. Chester said. Several girls from the other side of the gym looked over. Gymnastics was coed, which made the activity particularly embarrassing.

"Watch me first." Mr. Chester crouched down on all fours to show David how to position himself for a forward roll.

The girls pranced around in their blue uniforms, locker keys dangling from their wrists on red and white plastic braids. What soundless rhythm they moved to fascinated him—their easy laughter and the pleasure they took with their bodies turning somersaults and cartwheels in space.

"Pay attention, David," Mr. Chester said. He rolled forward and hit the front of the mat with a heavy thud.

David crouched down but couldn't make himself roll.

"I'll give you a push," Mr. Chester said. But as soon as he reached down, David jumped up and backed away.

"What's the matter, son?"

"I don't feel well," David said. The thought of being pushed over by Mr. Chester was frightening.

"You'll have to make the attempt," Mr. Chester said. "I can't pass you unless you make the attempt. There's nothing wrong with you and no reason why you can't do a forward roll. Everybody can do a forward roll."

"I'll go first," David's father said. Home from work for the first night all week, he had bought a mat to help David practice his gymnastics. David's mother stood against the wall in the rec room. His twelve-year-old sister, Tina, did flips, splits, cartwheels, handsprings. What a showoff, David thought.

Change fell out of his father's pocket when he did a lumpy roll across the mat. He stood up, red faced, his neck swelling over his collar. He was out of breath. "See? Nothing to it."

David's mother remained silent.

His father loved to watch sports on TV. He couldn't understand David's lack of interest and two years ago had forced David to try out for the junior high basketball team. After everyone did a set of layups, the coach took David aside and said he could be a manager. "A player manager?" David's father asked that evening when David told him what had happened. "That's terrific. Like Pete Rose—only in basketball, right?" David nodded because he didn't want to disappoint his father. But when the first game came and his father arrived wearing a red sweater, the school color, with a scorecard in hand, and sat in the second row behind the team, all he saw was his son conked on the head by one of the basketballs that David hustled to collect after the players' warmup. "You don't even suit up," his father said on the way home. He sounded disgusted. David sat with the players' sweaty towels in a gym bag on his lap. Part of his job was to take the smelly towels home after the game and wash them. He thought about how wringing wet they were, the ten pounds of sweat he had to lug back with him. "They don't let you suit up?"

"I'm not a player. I'm just a manager."

"Christ, they don't even let you suit up," his father repeated. "Maybe you could at least ask them to let you suit up."

The following summer he went to work as an errand boy in the accounting firm where his father was a senior partner. Fran, the head secretary, was always polite and respectful and called him Mr. Lorber, like his father. Bringing his father back a corned beef sandwich one day, he walked in on the two of them embracing and it was so upsetting for everyone that David began to laugh ghoulishly, the kind of laugh he had when he watched *A Creeper Feature* by himself on Friday nights and was scared out of his wits, and then he ran out of the office until his father chased him down.

"Your mother and I . . . we have some problems," he said to David, out of breath. "It isn't anything that can be helped."

"I don't want to work with you anymore," David said. "I don't want you to *push* me anymore."

"Of course, of course," his father said and David knew they had struck some kind of bargain, a bribe. His father could be made to squirm like everyone else. It was a sad revelation, the sudden power he had over him that made his father a frightened giant. "We don't need to tell anyone about this," his father said. David kept his face blank. He'd traded a piece of something solid and clean clutched deep inside him, something he had started out with, something everyone started out with. Gone now. "Promise?" David put his head down and nodded.

His father was on his hands and knees now, trying to align David's limbs for a forward roll. His mother stood above them, her hands spread over David's head, as though in a tense prayer. She couldn't stand noise of any kind—anyone else's noise. David was embarrassed to have friends over because she would shout down at them to Shut up, your yelling is driving me crazy!— when they weren't yelling at all, when they were playing quietly. The least disturbance from David or his sister produced hysterics way out of proportion to the wet towel left on the bathroom floor or the radio turned up too loud. He was frightened of his mother and tried always to be in a different part of the house than she was. In the morning he made sure he woke before she began slamming drawers or banging pots around in the kitchen, which happened all the time like some deranged percussion symphony. His sister, meanwhile, frozen with fear that she was somehow responsible for such rage, tried even harder to please but would collapse at the slightest criticism or disappointment—

if the peach in her lunch had a bruise on it. At twelve, she had already started wearing makeup and would stand in front of the mirror in the morning dabbing at her one or two pimples with cotton and alcohol. "That isn't good for your skin," David had warned her, trying to be helpful. Bad skin was an adolescent affliction he had been spared. "Please," she said with unbearable frustration at the intrusion. "I have to get this *done*." She was convinced if she only worked hard enough on the pimples she'd shrink them out of sight. David's heart went out to her, but his own frustration took the form of a chronic passivity and he just shrugged and walked past.

"Make your body into a tight ball and just roll." His father gripped David's shoulders, ready to throw him forward. At the other end of the mat was Wayne, their basset hound, his MY NAME IS WAYNE. PLEASE RETURN ME TO . . . and other tags jiggling from his collar as he tried to come forward, restrained by Tina, to slobber on David for good luck. The will of the entire family pressed down on him. He had to do this for them. If he failed gym, he failed tenth grade, he failed his family, he failed God, whose latest incarnation for David had taken the form of Q12081011, a newly discovered quasar 73 billion trillion miles from earth. He tried to picture how far away that was—as far as he would have to roll.

"One . . . two . . . "

He grabbed onto his father's knees. He grabbed on with such force that his father screamed out in pain.

"So," Rabbi Greenberg said. "You're wondering why I wanted to see you, David."

"No," David said. He knew why. His father had asked the rabbi to speak with him. He heard his father making the call after they gave up practicing gymnastics. *We can't do anything with him. He stays up all night and plays with that telescope we should never have given him. He mumbles when you ask him a question. And he's got some kind of phobia about gym class. Maybe you could just talk with him. He respects you. See what's up with him. We're ready to take him to a doctor, a psychiatrist, you know.* David had crept away from the closed bedroom door. He was becoming an expert at moving around the house with stealth. No one knew where he was, whether he was even home; no one could see him, he had become so adept at slipping around corners. Not bad for a mortal, he would say to himself as he disappeared behind a doorway, just missing being seen by his mother, father, or sister.

There were pictures on the wall of Rabbi Greenberg accepting an award from the United Jewish Appeal. Pictures of the rabbi, his wife, and daughter Leah in Israel. Pictures of the rabbi at a Purim celebration in the synagogue, waving a noisemaker, a huge smile jumping out from his gray beard. David remembered a conversation he'd had with the rabbi two years ago, right before he was bar mitzvahed and was reading obsessively about the Holocaust, a subject that haunted him until astronomy became a more abstract yet purer contemplation of heaven and hell.

"What would happen," the rabbi had said, making time to talk with him, the first adult who took him seriously, "if there were neither one?"

"You mean nothing afterward?"

"No. That I didn't say. Not nothing. I said if there were neither heaven nor hell."

"I'm sorry. I don't understand the question."

He didn't. It was hard enough to imagine nothing—like trying to take an egg apart, empty out the yolk, and put the shell back together. Inside there was not nothing but rather the missing egg . . . which still existed, even if it wasn't inside anymore; it was an egg missing its insides, an eggless egg.

"What else could there be then?"

"Let me put it to you this way," the rabbi said. "Suppose you have two rooms. One is blue. The other is blue. One has good, comfortable furniture. So does the other. One has a nice fruit basket on the coffee table. Funny thing, so does the other. You look closer, you see these two rooms are exactly the same, same color, same furniture, same size, same fruit basket, same temperature, same scratch on the wall. But you know one is heaven and one is hell! You've been told this. How do you know when you're in one you're not, in fact, sitting in the other?"

"That's easy," David said. There was a knock at the rabbi's door. He was glad when the rabbi told the person just a minute. "You tie a string from one to the other and follow it back and forth. Two objects can't occupy the same space at the same time. This proves their separate existence."

"Ah," the rabbi said and stood up to answer the door. He had put his hand on David's shoulder. "Maybe you're right." But David had gotten the impression that his response was the correct *wrong* answer, the one the rabbi had expected but not wanted.

"What have you been reading?" the rabbi said now.

"Astronomy."

"No more Holocaust literature?"

"Not right now."

"You have anyone to tell your thoughts? Teachers at school? Any smart friends?"

"No."

"I would have been interested."

"I didn't want to bother you," David said.

"You mean you didn't want me to bother you."

He supposed that was true. Everything he did now he thought of as secret. As soon as he came home from school, he locked his bedroom door, read his astonomy books until late at night and then took the lens cap off his telescope and tracked the progression of Sirius or Canopus or Arcturus and the loneliness vanished.

"So what's doing with you? You're going to let some nudnick gym teacher keep you from passing this year?"

He told the rabbi about the gymnastics class.

"Let me understand," he said. "He won't pass you in gym because you won't do a forward roll?"

"Can't. Yes."

"What kind of Minnie Mouse business is this!"

Rabbi Greenberg stood up and stormed around the office. David had never seen him so upset. Finally, he told David to go home, he would take care of this personally. David left a little in awe of the rabbi's wrath.

But later that evening, the rabbi called and told him the gym teacher just wanted to see David try, he was refusing even to try—or he would need a medical excuse, which might be arranged also.

"No," David said. "I prefer not to," he added, quoting a character he had liked in a story from his literature class.

"So," the rabbi said. "I see this is your choice, what you wish."

"I didn't think so. Maybe it is." He thought about the moon circling the earth, the earth circling the sun, the planets circling each other, the galaxy rotating round another galaxy, the entire universe passing through a white hole to another universe and all of it repeated ad infinitum on a microcosmic level with subatomic particles, nothing stable. "I won't do it," David said. "I won't roll forward."

Q12081011 shines as brightly as 500 galaxies yet is a fraction of the diameter, a mere light month across. The quasar is the most powerful known, capable in one hour of generating as much energy as the sun does in its entire lifetime. Distance is 73 billion trillion miles from earth. Moving at a speed of 36,000 miles per second away from us this makes the quasar a front runner at the edge of the expanding universe. If God wears a jewel in his forehead, this is it. I have felt myself waiting for a discovery of this power. If I could see it, see any part of its light . . .

David's sister knocked at his door. "What?"

"Open up."

"Why?"

"Please!"

David unlocked the door. Tina stood there in her school clothes—parrot green pants and an orange T-shirt hanging down one shoulder. She had just gotten home from the mall

where she went with her friends every afternoon to see boys
and play Whirly Ball. "Mom won't come out of her room."

"What are you talking about?"

"She won't come out. I tried calling to her that I was home
and she didn't answer."

"Maybe she's asleep."

"She isn't asleep. She never sleeps in the afternoon. You go
and see if you can get her to come out."

"Not me," David said. He backed away. The thought of en-
tering his mother's room unbidden scared him. He hardly spoke
to her as it was. They saw each other at dinner and in the
hallway only when he found it unavoidable. She was a ghost
or he was a ghost. Either way, the idea of knocking on her
locked bedroom door was out of the question.

"Leave her alone. She's just resting," David said, making himself believe it.

"Will you please *do* something?"

David shook his head.

"You make me so mad! You're so snotty about everything
because you can't even do a somersault in gym you're so spastic!"
They were back to this again. She was liable to say anything
now. He sat with his arm around the barrel of his telescope
and waited. "I hate you! I hate everyone in this family!"

David heard her running up and down the hallway, to no
apparent purpose. If anything was to get his mother out of her
room, this was sure to do it—noise.

But she didn't come out. And his sister returned and pleaded
with him to do something, please do something. Now, too,
Wayne came jiggling into his room and looked up at David with
bloodshot eyes.

David went down the hallway and took a few deep breaths
before knocking lightly on his mother's door. There was no
answer.

"What should we do?" his sister said. Her purple eyeshadow,
smeared from crying, was the color of eggplant.

He rested his hand on the doorknob; it turned. "Didn't you
try the door before?"

She shook her head. "I thought it was locked," she said, as surprised as he was. They spoke in whispers to each other.

He opened the door. His mother was sitting at the table where she had coffee every morning by the window. She was wearing her bathrobe. She must have been there since morning, David realized. "Mom?" he said. His sister looked over his shoulder. Wayne's uncut claws clicked across the wood floor, but even he stayed back. "Mom, are you okay?"

He walked closer and then touched her shoulder and looked at her face. It was empty, chalky pale in the light from the window. Her hair was flat against her right cheek as though she'd slept on it all night. Her bathrobe was open, and he turned away from her flaccid breasts. She said something, but too faintly to hear.

"What?" David said.

"I'm going to make dinner."

"Mom," his sister said. "What's *wrong* with you?"

"We'll have green beans tonight. Both of you children. Don't you? You both know green beans?"

Her voice was barely audible, the words at the tail end of a breath in a monotone that made him shiver.

"Watch her," he whispered to Tina, who stood against the wall, her eyes huge; she held on to Wayne and stared at their mother, who didn't move. "I'm going downstairs to call Dad."

In the kitchen, he dialed his father's office. The new secretary—Fran had left five months ago—asked if she could take a message. His father was in conference.

"This is his son."

"Oh, hi David."

"Could you interrupt him? It's important." He added "urgent," but she had already put him on hold.

"What's the matter, David?" His father's voice was quick, annoyed. It was his busiest time of the year. Two weeks before tax day, April 15.

"Something's wrong with Mom. She won't come out of the bedroom."

"What do you mean she won't come out of the bedroom? Is she lying down?"

"She's just sitting at the window. She's still in her bathrobe."

"Put her on."

"She can't talk."

"What's going on, David? Stop playing games and put your mother on the phone."

"I'm not playing games. Don't talk to me about playing games!" He was shouting. He cradled the phone under his chin and calmed himself. His temples pounded with blood and he could hear all the noise inside his head that his mother made in the mornings when she went on her drawer-slamming rampage. "If you're not home in a half-hour I'll tell everyone— everybody you ever met! I swear I will. You know what I'm talking about."

"David?"

"You better come home. That's all I got to say. If you don't come home . . . I swear if you don't come home . . . "

He hung up, then took the receiver off the hook so his father couldn't call back. He went upstairs. His mother and sister were as he had left them. "Is Dad coming?" Tina asked quickly.

"He'd better," David said. He sat down beside his mother. "Can I get you anything?" She didn't answer him. She started to move her lips, there was some spittle between her bottom teeth and lip, then she closed her mouth. She thought she had spoken.

David touched her palm, open flat in her lap. She let his finger lie there, then closed her hand around it. Tina was swallowing her tears. "Come here," he told her. She came over immediately. "Sit down next to us and hold onto Mom's other hand." She did so obediently, glad to be following orders. "Tell her what you did at school today."

"What?"

"Tell her anything."

His sister talked about a math quiz and planning her class's project for Ecology Day and the spicy burritos for lunch. He listened to her voice . . . how hard she was trying. Their mother began to cry silently. He thought about the new quasar, to know he might one day see it! But its light was 12.4 billion years old, just now reaching the earth—who could know if the quasar itself still existed? He felt his throat tighten in pain. His sister rushed on about choral practice and a fire drill at school and her friend Joan's spiked hair, and he held tight to his mother's hand and looked out the window with her and down at their world.

Summer of Love

The radio stations were calling 1967 the Summer of Love, but my father informed me it was to be a summer of work and made arrangements for me to be a waiter at my Aunt Letty's hotel in the Catskills. The lodge was near Liberty, New York, between the more famous resorts of Grossinger's and Brown's. After I flew from Ohio, where we lived and where I would be starting college in the fall, I took the bus from the Port Authority up to Liberty and then a cab from there to Aunt Letty's place, Hy-Sa-Na Lodge.

The hotel's driveway was a mile-long gravel road overhung with tree branches. The cab bumped along the single lane that narrowed with tall weeds brushing the windows and doors, until we came to a three-story lodge. Patio tables, their blue and white umbrellas folded, lined a veranda that ran along three sides of the hotel. The hotel, my father told me, warning me not to expect too much, had been a fashionable resort in its heyday, the Forties and Fifties, but over time, and with Letty's husband, my Uncle Bumin, dying years ago, the place had deteriorated.

I paid for my cab and went up the steps. The screen door had holes in it, and I saw that the paint on the walls was peeling. Fat pigeons cooed and dropped their feathers into crooked gutters. Aunt Letty stood behind the front desk, her hand shaking as she wrote. She had Parkinson's disease. I had not seen her since I was five, when she came out for my mother's funeral. She had kept me company, helped me color pictures of dinosaurs and whales and played quiet games with me while mourners came to our house to sit shivah. I was told my mother would be "in heaven missing me." Sadness collected in empty spaces I never knew existed in our house—places that I came to understand are always reserved for such grief.

"Ivan!" Aunt Letty said, looking up. "You're here!"

We hugged each other and Aunt Letty asked me did I want something to eat, a glass of milk, some tea? No, I said, I was fine. It was just nice to be here.

"I hope you won't be too lonely up here, Ivan."

"Are there any other waiters?" I had come a week early; the season officially opened on Memorial Day.

"Two," Aunt Letty said. "They'll come soon. One is from Connecticut, and the other is a young man from Long Island. Both seem such nice gentlemen. The young man from Long Island wrote me a long letter about his military background and training. He sounded very responsible."

It didn't sound good to me. I'd gone on a chartered bus to Washington to march against the war, and I'd turned down a scholarship to Purdue University because R.O.T.C. was required.

"What military school is he from?"

"West Point, I believe."

"West Point!" Even I could be impressed by West Point.

"Ivan, I don't know if your father told you, but many of our guests are older here. I hope this won't bother you."

"Of course not."

"Some are very old."

"I like being around older people, Aunt Letty."

"Good. You'll let me know if there's anything you need. I want you to be happy up here. I so loved your mother. She was my favorite cousin when we were children."

"Yes," I said. "She thought a lot of you, too," although I didn't know this for sure. I was used to making up a personality for my mother since she had died when I was so young.

Aunt Letty smiled. Her teeth were square, conspicuously false. "I try to keep up the place, Ivan, but it's so hard by myself.

And we just don't have the funds that we used to." Her voice
rose nervously when she said "funds." "I don't think we can go
on for too long the way things are now. We have our regulars
but less and less come back every summer. And now, the young
people, with their new ways, the long hair and all this trouble
about the war and the riots in the cities, who understands any
of this?" I sat and listened politely and then Aunt Letty said,
"I'm rambling, Ivan. Please don't let me do that. Come, I'll show
you where you will sleep, darling."

A hundred yards up a dirt path, the old recreation hall once
showcased the big bands and comedians who played the borscht
belt. Now the building housed only bats and mice and an occasional opossum. Aunt Letty had offered me a private room
in the main lodge, but I didn't want special treatment, so I chose
a room in the back of the recreation hall, one where other waiters
in years past had carved their moment in history on the lodge's
walls: Lewis Goldberg ZBT, 1962; Mike Michaelson, Hofstra
University, 1950; Miss Lucy Fishman and Mr. Barry Weinstein
slept here, 1947. I moved the rickety card tables out of the
room, swept the floor, covered the missing pane in the window
with cardboard so the mosquitoes wouldn't eat me alive, and
set a clock up on a conga drum that I'd found behind the stage.
    During the day, dust would swirl in the light that streamed
through the splintered rafters of the ballroom and cobwebs
would glisten silver, but I could imagine the dances and shows
and gala parties that had once taken place here, the orchestra
on stage, the drummer swishing his brushes, the droll bassman,
and then—a sudden change in tempo—the band leader puts
aside his trumpet and beats a tattoo on this conga drum, while
my mother and father and their friends do a steamy rhumba.
I missed my own music now. The small radio I'd brought up
got poor reception in the mountains and the two Beatles records
I had gingerly transported had nowhere to be played. At night,
I'd lie awake for a long time and listen to the bats in the ballroom, their wings flapping. I'd imagine their furry bodies and

crinkled faces and red eyes and razor teeth—their radar pinging off my head. Once, when I couldn't stand it anymore and turned on the light to see, a group of ten or so swooped like a single large and reptilian wing from one end of the ballroom to the other—then shot back into the rafters. After that, I always left the light on and pulled the covers over my head to sleep. In the morning, with the bright sunshine, all would be quiet, the bats back in their holes, the mountains green and smelling of wild lilac and mint, the air cold and the grass dewy, the smoke rolling up from the kitchen's chimney as I walked down the dirt path to eat breakfast.

I was alone for a week, and during that time I helped Aunt Letty set up the dining room. I polished the silver, inventoried the dishes (meat and dairy plates—I had to learn about kosher service), separated the worn linens, filled salt and pepper shakers, and shampooed the carpet in the dining room. At the end of the week, Lester Malmar arrived. He threw his duffle bag down on the bed in the recreation hall's long front room. He opened the bag, took out white cadet gloves, and placed them carefully on the room's dresser. He was tall, with black curly hair, but I thought a little overweight for a West Point cadet. His legs were especially flabby, his skin pale under the hair. His sandals were held together with electrical tape.

"Where you going to college?" he asked me.

"Ohio University," I said.

"Major?"

"Psychology."

"In Russia you'd be insane."

I realized, with a sinking feeling, that I'd have to go through the whole summer with Lester Malmar.

"That's what they call people over there who don't believe in Marx's little red book."

"Mao's," I corrected.

"Hold the Mao!" Lester roared. He laid an attaché case on the bed, popped open the snaps and lifted the lid. Inside was a pistol.

"Don't worry, it's not loaded. I keep the bullets separate. That's one thing they teach us in weapons class—firearm safety. You want to do some target practice sometime? I'll show you how to shoot."

"No thanks."

"There's plenty of places around here."

"I hate guns."

"Suit yourself." Then Lester flopped on the bed and laid the gun tenderly on his stomach. He lit a cigar, something else I detested.

What saved me from Lester was Jeff showing up the next day. Jeff brought his stereo with him and a terrific collection of records. He wore rose-tinted granny glasses, a rope belt of bells, silver studs along the seams of his jeans, and baggy white shirts from Mexico with bright embroidery. His hair, wavy brown and parted in the middle, came over his ears, and with his dark lashes, brown eyes, and wide mouth he looked like a cross between George Harrison and Paul McCartney. It didn't hurt the resemblance that he played guitar and sang in a band, and that his voice, deep and rich, could fill the entire recreation hall. The weekend after he moved in, he brought back a date from town and set a chair for the girl in the middle of the dance floor. On stage, he entertained her, a cappella, with Elvis, Roy Orbison, Jerry Lee Lewis. His encore, to the wild applause of us all, had been Gerry and the Pacemakers' "Don't Let the Sun Catch You Crying," and he had crooned the song in such dulcet, plaintive, and heart-seizing notes that his date, a first date, leaped up at the end and shouted, "Marry me!"

I hoped I would meet someone, too, that summer. But there were no girls at the hotel. Aunt Letty had been right: all the guests were old, and canes were prominent. I had to remember to speak up when waiting on my people, and to make sure I saved a piece of Nova lox for Mrs. Shlotzky, and that even if Mr. Edleman wanted a Danish not to give it to him (his fifty-year-old daughter had warned me) because he was a diabetic, and to always bring Mrs. Fine "a little hot water with lemon, please—hot, please, bubeleh, hot," and to remember that Mr. Wallach had a "reaction" to the kosher dairy substitute for cream and so I was to empty out the kosher substitute and put in plain milk, though never to tell Mr. Wallach this because he would die of a heart attack if he knew, and to Mr. Rosen give no salad because the roughage "makes my ulcer grab like a python."

At the end of the week, they would each call me over, on the porch or outside where they'd be walking slowly up and down the driveway, with their large sun hats, their white summer shoes, dark socks and plaid shorts. A five-dollar bill would be crushed into my hand. "So good you are," they'd say, or "So you should go to college and be as good a doctor as a waiter," or "Please, next time, a little hotter the water, hot, bubeleh."

One day in early July, Jeff and I walked down the road to the Brown's Hotel. Brown's was famous for Jerry Lewis—they'd named their nightclub after him—who had once worked at the resort as a busboy. Jeff had said, "Let's go in the lounge for a drink." I agreed, although it made me nervous. I had turned eighteen in April and only drank 3.2 beer in Ohio, which I knew was not sold around here. So I ordered what Jeff did, which was a shot of tequila. Although I remained perfectly composed on the outside, a flame like a gas derrick's shot through my stomach.

I turned in my chair to watch Jeff, who had gone over to the large windows that bordered the pool. He tapped on the glass at two girls outside in bikinis, motioning them to come inside. I panicked. I couldn't believe he was doing this to me.

They told him to come outside instead.

Jeff walked back to where I was sitting. "Let's go talk to them," he said.

"Do you know them?"

"No. Should I?"

His voice had already dropped into that chocolatey, deep register he used for singing and talking to girls.

"I can't, Jeff."

"Why not?"

He looked at me as if it would never occur to him that such a thing as shyness existed in the world. With his good looks, his bedroom eyes, his easy words, his light curls—what would he know about a choked voice, sweaty hands, a heartbeat loud as a cowbell? The girls weren't going to be interested in me, serious, analytical, preoccupied with the war, not to mention skinny legs and the rash on them from some weeds we had tromped through on our way here.

"I can't go out there." I just couldn't imagine how. The girls in their bikinis: the light catching the necklace in the taller girl's cleavage, their slick, wet hair and golden shoulders, their eager hand signals to Jeff, their fingernails pink and sharp against the glass . . . how experienced they looked through the window. The tequila, rather than relaxing me, raced through my system and melted connective tissue, my will oozing out like sloppy airplane glue.

"I'll help you," Jeff said. "I won't leave you hanging." He put his hand on my shoulder. Here was a leader, I thought, here was somebody who could get men up a hill into battle.

"You talk with them by yourself. Really, it's okay. I'm just not in the mood," I lied.

Jeff sat down next to me at the bar. He studied me for a minute, then said, "No big deal. There will be lots of other chances. You ready to go back?"

"Yes," I said, immensely grateful that he hadn't taken my suggestion and left me.

Although I'd had a girlfriend in Ohio, we had broken up before I left for Aunt Letty's hotel. Elise thought making the separation official would be a good idea since we were going to different colleges anyway and she wanted to be free. We had slept together twice, near the end of the school year, but there was something too quiet and mechanical about it, as though we were taking turns touching each other rather than making love, all mixed up and wild. She'd held me in such a peculiar way, more as if to contain me than embrace me. I had been glad to be going away for the summer.

After a while Jeff stopped asking me to visit other hotels with him and instead took Lester. They would come back late at night, loud and drunk, pounding my bed, wanting me to wake up and share the rest of the wine or vodka or tequila or beer. Once, they both returned with girls. I pulled the covers over my head and waited. Then it started: the rustling of clothes, the sound of zippers, the dropping of change, the giggling, the squeaking of bedsprings, the moaning.

I stayed awake long after everyone became quiet.

Aunt Letty had asked me to watch the desk while she went to talk with the chef. A cab stopped outside and instead of a shaky foot and orthopedic shoe touching the ground, out jumped a young girl wearing jeans and a blue workshirt with her hair in a long brown braid.

I opened the screen door for her and asked if I could help. She looked me up and down, at my red vest and black butterfly bow tie and the ruffled white shirts we wore to serve dinner, then at my polished shoes, and said, "You're Ivan, I bet."

"How did you know?"

"I'm Maida, Letty's granddaughter."

"Oh," I said. "Nice to meet you." We shook hands and her fingers curled around mine, kindly, with affection. Her face was open and friendly and I immediately relaxed. I was even able to joke about her suitcase, tied together with twine and taped in the corners. "Did you drag that behind the cab?"

Maida laughed and said she liked it because it had belonged to her father, who had taken it everywhere with him. He had loved to travel.

The logical question would have been, Do you like to travel, too? But for some reason I asked about her father.

"Is your father dead?" I said. I don't know why. Maybe I'd heard it from my father. My mother had been Maida's father's second cousin, which (and I was calculating quickly) made Maida and me distant relations, but close enough to be curious about each other.

What happened, however, in that first moment was one of those glitches of conversation when the unexpected remark or question becomes the truest one and a clumsy bump turns the world right side up. "Yes, he's dead," Maida said. "He killed himself." I nodded and took her hand again. I remembered now I knew this. Then I picked up her father's battered suitcase and we went to find Letty.

Maida and I began spending all our free time together. We'd swim or take long walks between my serving meals and then, at night, we'd sit on the porch and talk until late. When it was my evening to work the card room, she helped me serve tea and coffee. All the guests fussed over her and said, "Come, Maida, sit with us, darling." She would kiss the men's cards for good luck or pretend to know which ones they should throw down. Thursday evening was music night. Nathan the Piano Man, who toured the smaller resorts, would appear promptly at eight. With a dreamy smile, the suggestion of misunderstood genius about his eyes, the faint proudness of a man who could not endanger his hands by changing a tire or touching a hot plate, he would play ancient, moody melodies. Maida would stand with her arm through Letty's and they would sing "Rosie" together, as Letty used to do with Uncle Bumin.

I wanted to learn everything about Maida, and about her side of the family, which I didn't know well, my mother's family. I told Maida about my mother, what a shadowy figure she had been for me and how I didn't remember her too clearly even though I was already five when she died.

"Maybe it's too hard to remember," she said.

We were sitting on the porch steps of the recreation hall and I was picking at the rotten wood. I had a hard time talking about my mother, knowing what to say or what people expected me to say.

"Why didn't your father remarry?" Maida asked.

"I don't know why. He was pretty busy with his law firm. He tried with me. We'd go on camping trips in the summer and he'd come home from work to check on me when I got back from school in the afternoon. But I always felt he was as lonely as I was. I was aware we were different from other families, flying on one wing, so to speak." I paused, then said, "I thought that if I'd had a brother or a sister things would have been easier."

"Well, you have a cousin," Maida said.

She put her hand on my knee. I leaned over and kissed her. I felt her mouth open wide and the blood rush to my fingertips touching her cheek. Elise had never kissed me with her mouth open or pushed her tongue inside. I pulled away. "Is this all right?" I asked.

"Of course, silly."

"I mean about us being cousins. I think we're third cousins."

"Who's counting," Maida said and cupped my neck, pulling my face back into hers.

Maida would come up behind me in the dining room and put her arms around me, whisper to meet her upstairs (in her room) the minute I finished serving. She'd be waiting for me. But if I showed up unexpectedly, she'd be agitated, upset, as if she didn't want me there, pacing around the room or telling me she had to finish writing a letter or reading a novel. Any display of passion I initiated was gently but clearly rebuffed. I'd rack my brain as to what I'd done wrong. Finally, one day, I just came out and asked her why she never let me surprise her. We had taken out the sole canoe to the middle of the lake and were drifting slowly back toward the shore, a stem of fat grapes between us that we'd grabbed over the screaming protest of the hotel's Chinese pantry man.

"I don't know," Maida said, pulling away from me. She'd been lying against my shoulder. She sat now in the middle of the boat, facing me. Wearing one of my shirts over her bathing suit, so her shoulders wouldn't burn, she had tied the tails in a bow across her stomach. The down on her arms had turned almost white from the sun. "I just like my privacy."

"But you come to my room all the time," I said.

"You told me I could. You said you *liked* to be surprised."

"It's more than that," I said. "You always have to be in charge, don't you?"

"What makes you say that?" Maida smiled and pushed a finger against my chest, leaving a white spot in the center. "Can't we just stop talking about this? It's so boring, Ivan."

"You're not bored with anything else we talk about. Why this?"

"Maybe you should be a lawyer instead of a psychologist."

"Maybe you should be an evasive witness."

Maida sighed with great, heaving annoyance. "Okay, so I don't like surprises. Is that any big deal?"

A fish jumped in the water. The lake was overflowing with trout but there was no one to fish. Only eighty-six-year-old Mr. Wallach, Hy-Sa-Na Lodge's oldest guest, came up here occasionally in his chest waders.

Maida scraped her sneaker back and forth against the bottom of the canoe. "Ivan . . ."

"What?"

"Come over here. I want to tell you something." I slid over to where Maida was sitting. "Come closer. It's a secret." She wrapped her arms around my neck and pulled me into the water. We floated around down there while she held tight to my neck, and for a moment I thought her secret was going to be that we would drown together.

Jeff was a regular topic of conversation between Maida and me. Maida didn't share my admiration for him, nor find him nearly as charming as I did.

"Oh, look at him, will you, Ivan? He can't even talk to women without coming on to them."

"Which women?"

"Me! He's constantly fluttering his eyelashes—he might as well have a motor behind them. And buzzing in that bee voice of his."

"I love his voice!"

"It reminds me of runny marmalade."

"Why do you dislike him so much? What's he ever done to you?"

"Nothing. He just bothers me. That car he bought." Jeff had spent his money from the summer so far on a '63 Triumph, while I carefully deposited mine at a bank in Liberty.

"It's his choice," I said. "Why should he have to be practical if he doesn't want?"

"It's his attitude, that he's so clever and cute. What's he going to do next year? Is his sporty little car going to save him? I tried to talk to him about going to college, just for a year to buy himself some time. No, he wouldn't think of it. He's not going to hide behind some pompous professor's robes, he told me. I mean, come on, it's one thing to make a point on principle, but that's not his reason. He's just acting out some juvenile rebellion against his father."

"His father! How do you know this?" Jeff had never mentioned anything to me about his father.

"His dad is a big corporate executive who wants Jeff to follow in his footsteps, go to Stanford like he did."

"I'm amazed he told you all this."

"That's what I mean. He tells me all these things because he thinks I'm just naturally interested in his life—wouldn't any girl be? It's his tone. He was actually explaining, in boring detail, how to do the backstroke in the pool."

"Well, he was on his school's swim team."

"So was *I*."

"I think you're too hard on him, Maida."

"And I think he's the brother you always wanted. He can't do much wrong in your eyes."

"Maybe," I said, feeling suddenly caught.

Still, Jeff had the only car and it forced the three of us together. Lester was left out, mostly, we told ourselves, because we took the Triumph and there wasn't room for him. It became embarrassing to sneak away, for that's what it felt like, a quick goodbye and then we'd hurry down the steps, leaving Lester on the porch squeezing a handgrip and looking after us with a stern military grimace. One evening we came home late and found Lester

wearing his cadet uniform, with white-gloved hands behind his
back, standing in front of a map of the world he'd mounted on
his wall. Besides listening to military marches and famous nar-
rations of great battles, he plotted troop movements, his troops,
in the Vietnam war. Tonight the allies (the blue pins) had invaded
every communist country except, as far as I could see, Russia.
Jeff went straight to bed. Lester and I remained side by side
facing his map. "It was a hell of a war," he said.

"Was?"

He nodded at the map. His face had broken out in hives the
last few days but only the left side; the smooth right side was
cleanly shaved. The doctor had told him not to shave the other
side until the rash cleared up. The smooth profile was toward
me. I tried to follow his gaze. "What are you nodding at?"

He pointed at Russia.

"Yes," I said. "No blue pins. Why?"

Lester turned his full face toward me now—the rashy, hairy,
left side and the clean-shaven right. "It doesn't exist. I've elim-
inated the problem."

"I'm going to bed," I said.

"You can run but you can't hide."

"Figure it all out, Lester, and let me know in the morning
what happens to the world."

"I feel sorry for you, Ivan Ivanovitch! I had such hope for
you when I first came here. You seemed intelligent, if
misguided."

"Give me a break."

"Give yourself a break and wake up, man!"

"Shut up!" Jeff shouted from his room.

"And him, they'll break him in two minutes. The bamboo
shoots under his fingernails, the leeches on his testicles, the
grains of rice soaked in urine and ground into the razor cuts
on the bottoms of his feet. He'll be begging for the bullet through
his head."

"Where do you think of this stuff, Lester?"

"Read Tom Dooley, my friend. Tortures beyond our minds."

I started to walk away. Lester called after me. "Wait a second, I want to tell you something."

"What?"

"I've conquered sleep."

"Mazel tov."

"Fatigue," Lester said. "Fatigue is the enemy." He smiled at me. "Why don't you join me—if you think you can take it. Unless you want to crawl into your bed, a wasted hophead like your fellow traveler in there."

"Hophead?"

"Go ahead. Smoke yourself into oblivion. Wake up with a bayonet in your soft white gut!"

Jeff appeared in the doorway. He was scratching his crotch and squinting through sleep at us. "Look, man, can you please keep it down? Go outside and talk at least."

Lester pulled his heels together, thrust out his chest. "Request denied! Recruit Jeffrey Jeffvanovitch will not cross the demarcated line of Captain Malmar's quarters!"

"You are such a retread," Jeff said and turned around, shuffling back to his room.

The next day I told Maida.

"He sounds sick. He really gives me the creeps."

"Should we tell Letty?" I asked.

"I don't know. He hasn't done anything wrong. He's just acting so weird."

Maida didn't like to be around Lester and would avoid the recreation hall if she knew he was there. He called her "Ma'am," as he addressed Letty and anyone in a postion of authority; he assumed Maida to be a superior because she was Letty's granddaughter.

"I catch him staring at me sometimes. But it's not as though he turns away when I meet his eyes. He keeps looking, Ivan." I rested my head in Maida's lap and kissed her smooth belly, her salty skin warm on my mouth. We'd come up to her room after lunch. "He's really not sleeping anymore?"

"That's what he says. Maybe he takes naps. How else can he stay awake?"

"Is he serving his guests all right?"

"Seems to be. He's always there—on both feet. He takes their orders, brings their food, then stands at attention by his coffee service, his chin up, until the last guest has left. He cleans up and goes back to the recreation hall."

"Maybe he sleeps then."

"No, that's when he polishes his shoes and cleans his gun."

"Gun! What do you mean, gun!"

"He has a pistol. Issued to him at West Point."

"They don't give out *handguns!*"

"How do you know?"

"They just don't." Maida got off the bed and went over to her dormer window. She put on a T-shirt and hugged herself. I came over to the window and held her. Her whole body was trembling.

"Are you okay?"

"No, I'm not okay. Do I look okay?"

"Well, don't get mad at me. I didn't bring him here."

Maida looked at me strangely, as if she didn't know who I was or couldn't trust me anymore. Later, I learned she had seen her father shoot himself.

I should say I was stoned during much of the summer. But whereas I would want to lie on my back and enjoy the effects of my circumlocution—stringing long words together and watching them spin off protoplasmically toward the stars, Maida wanted to fuck. Sex was what interested her most about grass. My brain's busy catwalks, which Maida was willing to traverse when we were straight, annoyed and scared her when we were stoned. "Don't talk like that, Ivan," she might say, or "Everything's getting too complicated and chopped up in my head." She didn't like me to tease her either, or talk in funny voices or do scary things like hold the flashlight under my chin and roll my eyes back. I reminded her too much of her father when I was stoned.

He'd been diagnosed as manic-depressive many years ago. In his manic phase he would stay up all night making phone calls to radio talk shows or friends if they would listen or, when there was no one else, all-night grocery stores to ask if they had a certain cereal or brand of tuna that he thought they should be carrying. In the morning, he'd be waiting at the bottom of the steps for Maida, telling her how to dress for school, which part to try out for in the class play, what to eat for lunch to keep her figure, leaping from one subject to another. He'd have gone over all her homework and commented on the teacher's comments. In high school, she had taken a course in shorthand; it wasn't unusual for him suddenly to clap his hands while they were watching TV (he would watch TV standing up) and command, "Maida, take a letter! To William Lensenk, Director, Royal Shakespeare Company. Dear Bill, Recently saw your production of *Richard III* on PBS and was ferociously disappointed. In Act I, Scene 3, Richard is *not* downstage. How can this be? To hide Richard at such a vital moment as this!"

Her father had been an actor and then a director of a reputable theater in New York before the war, where he had met Maida's mother. But he never achieved the recognition he thought he deserved, and he spent his life working as a salesman for a theater supply store in Manhattan. When he was depressed he couldn't work and once, refusing to eat or take care of himself in the most basic ways, he had been hospitalized. In the early Sixties he had been put on lithium and this helped him function normally enough to work. But as time passed and he showed no extreme swings of behavior, he claimed he was completely cured and no longer needed the medication. One night he was working at his desk, writing a play, his first attempt in years. Maida, sixteen and talking with a girlfriend in the living room, always with an ear out for her father's sudden shifts in mood, heard the typing stop, the only time his relentless pecking had ceased all night. She listened to him pull a page from the carriage, heard his sharp laugh and then went to see how he was doing. He pulled the trigger as she walked in the door. No one even knew he had a gun.

One would think (yes, one would think, I have said to myself many times looking back on that summer), knowing all this about Maida I wouldn't have pressured her into taking LSD. "Aren't you even curious?" I asked her.

"I'm scared. And, yes, of course I'm curious. You know I'm not a timid person. I just know it's bad for me."

This sounded perfectly reasonable, but still I persisted. "My first time I want you to be with me. We could take it Sunday, right after lunch." We didn't have to work Sunday evenings.

"I don't know. Let me think about it, Ivan."

Jeff would get us the LSD and guide us through the trip; he had taken acid several times already and swore by its powers.

"What's it like?" I had asked him.

"It has to be experienced," he said. "You can't explain an acid trip in words."

Which didn't sit well with me, since words had become an obsessive pursuit and I'd already filled four steno pads full of new vocabulary. The longer the better. If it had five syllables, a Latin derivation, and could be dragged from one's mouth like a wall of computers, I would work it into a conversation with Maida. "Your father longed to be a symposiarch," or "What tremendous vox angelica!" (about the final note on *Sgt. Pepper's*). I suppose Maida tolerated this as best she could. I thought I was speaking with clarity and precision and that my words would bring forth substance and color from an otherwise dull mind—my secret fear about myself then. "Why can't you talk in simple language and let your ideas stand on their own?" Maida would ask.

"Form is ideation. And language is the form overarching all other modes of human perception—mathematics, art, prayer. If there's no experimentation with language, there's no evolution in our awareness and the culture of ideas ceases to grow. And besides that, it's just fun."

"It's not very much fun for me. I have to keep a dictionary in my hand if I want to understand you."

"No need," I retorted. "I shall promulge a translation at your request."

Yes, where does arrogance like this come from? And how does anyone get away with it?

Maida agreed to take LSD with me near the end of the summer. I had finally said to her (in the most simple language possible), "It would mean everything to me if you did," implying that what "it" would mean is that if she truly loved me she would agree to do this, despite her fears. "It" had become something else, not the usual male plea for sex, but a new pressure. Maida's inner life. If I had this, I'd never lose her.

I asked Lester if he wanted to join us. And once I had extended the invitation, we were stuck with his acceptance.

Maida was speechless.

"I never expected him to say yes," I said.

"Why did you ask him then?"

I shrugged. I had an answer but I was embarrassed to tell her. We'd stopped halfway up the path to the recreation hall. Jeff was back there setting up, whatever that meant. "I thought he might feel more included."

"In *this*? Of all things, Ivan. Couldn't we just have gone to a movie with him if you were feeling guilty? Did you have to invite him on an acid trip with us?"

"I thought it would make him more . . . open."

"To what?"

"Maida, I'm trying to explain. You're not giving me a chance."

"You could have asked me first."

"I thought you would agree with me."

"About what?"

"That it might help him. Soften him up some." I turned away, embarrassed at what I wanted to say. "Help him love."

Maida sniffed my clothes. "God, Ivan, you reek of pot."

"I don't believe we can be at peace in the world until we find our enemy in here." I tapped my heart. "And until we stop hating one another. It seemed a good opportunity to practice that philosophy in my own backyard—with Lester."

"I'm getting sick."

"Look, you don't have to agree with me to respect an opinion."

"No, I'm really getting sick." Maida stepped to the side of the path and bent over. I held her hand while she took some

deep breaths and recovered. With the handkerchief from my
waiter's jacket I wiped the sweat from her face. "I feel better,"
she said. "It's going to be so crazy anyway, what's it matter?
I'm really nervous about this, Ivan. Just don't leave me."

Wearing a blue satin robe, sandals, and a leather choker, Jeff
greeted us at the door. "Peace and welcome," he said. He led
us into his bedroom. There, in a corner, with sandals also, sat
Lester. He saluted us.

"Hi," I said. "Getting comfortable?"

Lester nodded. "Just going along for the ride. I don't expect
anything can happen to me. Not if I don't let it. It's good training
to resist brainwashing, in case I ever get shot down."

Jeff handed me sandals. "Passengers will please remove their
shoes." I could see he was making an effort to ignore Lester.
Only after I'd convinced him that Lester would be less trouble
if he was with us instead of marching up and down in his room
playing John Philip Sousa marches or threatening to call the
cops did he agree to get an extra tab for him.

"Sit down," Jeff said. He'd brought all the pillows in from
the other rooms and spread them around the floor. On a foot-
high shelf was a bowl of marbles and a prism. "To look at
later," Jeff said. The stereo speakers stood at either end of the
shelf and on the speakers incense burned in brass holders.

Maida said, "Can't I just take off my sneakers? Do I have to
put sandals on?"

"Please," said Jeff. "We must be wearing the same materials
on our feet for our energy to connect."

"Those are flipflops," Maida said. "They're from Wool-
worth's."

"They are holy launching pads. Just put the goddamn things
on." Jeff smiled, politely. He'd been planning our trip for a week
now and didn't like his script being ruined. He gave us each a
stick of incense to hold. Lester sniffed his. Jeff coaxed us into
a circle in the middle of the floor and told us to join hands.
Lester reluctantly put his hand in mine but squeezed it extra
hard once he did, so he wouldn't be accused of having a limp

grip, I guess. I could barely restrain a yell. Jeff said, "Brothers and sisters, let freedom ring." Then he went over to his dresser, opened a drawer, and took out a plate covered with a handkerchief. It was a plate from the kitchen. He carried it over to us carefully, as though it were filled with water. When he set it down in front of us, there were four of the tiniest blue pills I'd ever seen.

"I don't want to go first," Maida said.

"I will," Lester volunteered. Jeff brought the plate over to him and he picked up the little pill—it looked harmless, almost cute—between his big thumb and forefinger, sniffed this too, then, placing it on the tip of his tongue so we all could see, rolled it down his throat. He held his hands out. See? Nothing to it.

"It takes about an hour to get off," Jeff said.

"Sure, tell me when we get there." Lester leaned back against the wall, closed his eyes, and snored. I avoided looking at Maida.

"Next?" Jeff said.

"Could I have a glass of water? I can't take a pill without water." I couldn't. Even the smallest tablet could make me choke.

Maida said she'd get me one, then came back with a cup of water from the bathroom and sat down next to me. She put her hand on my leg. "I want to take mine with Ivan."

So we did, swallowed them together, then kissed. Lester yawned audibly, followed by a snort. He was reading a car magazine.

I tapped Maida's shoulder, pointed out the window. "Isn't that Mrs. Bloom?"

"Where!"

"Coming toward us—in the hoop skirt and Living Bra."

Maida punched me.

"And there's Mr. Copperwas. I can read his lips. *Acid Schmacid.*"

"Don't you dare do this once we're off, Ivan. I'm not kidding."

"I promise. It's going to be fun."

Lester had his size twelve feet up on the wall and was turning pages as though he were ripping them out. Jeff danced around the room waving sticks of strawberry incense. He'd wrapped an Indian sari over his shoulders and was making wa wa noises. I checked my watch: 2:00 exactly. I felt great.

2:10 Maida gets up to use the bathroom. Jeff comes over to sit beside me. He sings in my ear, "You've got to admit it's getting better, it's getting better all the time . . . "

2:25 Lester is really sleeping. Or pretending so hard that he's convinced us all. He's curled in the fetal positon, snoring, his big body beached in the corner with his hands pressed between his knees. The hair on his chest sprouts from the collar of a green army T-shirt. I feel chilly and ask Jeff if this is a sign of getting off. He says not necessarily, but brings me a blanket from his bed. Maida asks me if I want some grape juice. "Sure," I say. "Do we have any?" She looks at me, confused by her own remark. "No, why did I think we did?" she says and we both break up laughing.

2:36 I have to go to the bathroom. Ordinarily I'd just get up and go, but I feel stuck. I'm suddenly worried I can't move and that this is the wrong thing to be doing. Maida is searching through her big straw bag for a pen. I've asked her for a better pen than the one I have, which is leaking all over my hand, stubby black ink dots. I have to continue making notes. She's taking all the things out of her bag and lining them up in neat soldier rows in front of her: keys, sunglasses, comb, brush, tampons, eyedrops, nail clippers, chapstick, postcards, matches, checkbook, photobooth pictures of us . . .
"I'll be right back," I say.
Maida looks up from her bag, her hand buried deep in the bottom. "What?"
"I said I'm just going to the bathroom for a minute."
"'kay," she says in a little girl's voice and goes back to rooting through her bag.

2:50 When I come back Maida is sitting crosslegged on the floor and the articles have multiplied into four rows.

"Did you find one?" I ask.

"One what?"

"A pen."

Maida rocks forward until her head touches the floor. She turns her cheek and looks up at me, smiling. "I*van*."

"What?"

"I*van,* come down here."

I sit down. Maida's rear is in the air and she's kneeling on the floor, her face in her hands. Her cheeks are red and her eyes are pushed back so she looks Chinese, or maybe it's Japanese. Or Austrian. Who knows. Jeff and Lester (who has "woken up") have gone to the hotel kitchen to get some food in case we get hungry later. I estimate and make a note that they have left "in tandem at 2:48."

Maida tugs on my arm while I write. "Stop, Ivan. Come down here and play."

"I have to write, Maida."

"Write what?"

"Everything. I need to keep a log. For instance, if you were to look directly overhead"—Maida drops her head back—"and could see through the roof of this building, you'd notice that the sun is directly above us and forms an exact perpendicular angle with the plane of your legs. This is called the angle of incidence. If we are on a hillside now . . . imagine that we are on a sand dune in the Sahara—"

"We're eating guava fruit."

"Right. And as we sit on this dune, its angle very slowly increases in steepness, growing more precipitous, until the moment we begin to slide down—that's the angle of repose."

"Angle of repose," Maida repeats, her eyes still closed. "I see lazy people with fat stomachs. They've wrapped themselves in cool white sheets and are stuffing guava fruit in their mouths. What is guava fruit, anyway?"

"I don't know."

"It tastes delicious, though," Maida says.

"What's it taste like?"

"Green."

"Sounds slimy."

"Not that kind of green, Ivan. The color of twilight. You stopped writing."

"Yes." I was turning my hand over, looking at the back and front, watching the veins.

"Want to make love?"

"Jeff and Lester will be back soon. Where?"

"In your room. We can lock the door."

"I'd feel funny with them out here."

Maida pulls at her T-shirt. "God, I really want to take off my clothes. Do you want to go swimming in the lake?"

I pick up my pen. The fact that it's leaked all over my hand no longer bothers me; it interests me. "I don't think that would be a good idea, under the circumstances."

"I just feel so hyper. I want to do something physical. Is this what's supposed to happen? All this antsyness?"

"I don't know. Maybe we should ask Jeff."

Who had walked through the door at the moment. Lester and he were carrying cheese, bread, fruit. I had no appetite.

Jeff brought a bottle of Welch's Grape Juice over to Maida. "Is this what you wanted?"

"Where'd you get it!"

"Never you mind, my princess." With a courtly bow he took a wine glass from his back pocket, unscrewed the bottle's top, poured a little grape juice in the glass and handed it to Maida. She sipped the juice, smacked her lips prettily.

"Does it meet with your approval?"

"Exquisite."

"And you?"

"What about me?" I said.

"Are you going to sit there until the cement dries around your butt?"

"I'm very comfortable." I picked up my notepad.

"He's keeping a log," Maida said.

"I see."

"Aren't you hot?" Maida said to Jeff.

"Yes."

"Want to swim?"

"Sounds great," Jeff said. He came over to me, walked around. I was sitting on my knees, my spine straight. Now that I was in this position even the slightest movement seemed extravagant. I was more interested in thinking about moving than actually moving. The body was an antiquated organism, primitive and unevolved. While thoughts could travel instantaneously, bodily parts followed behind like slow beetles.

Jeff lit a cigarette. He waved it in front of me. "See anything?"

"Your cigarette," I said. "What should I see?"

He made a wand of the burning ash and created loops, figure eights, fancy bows and spinning corkscrews.

"Wow," Maida said.

I restrained myself. I, too, saw the orange plumes from this tiny comet, but why should I cooperate? My thoughts were what interested me. Not these jokes for the eyes.

"I don't think we should leave this guy," Jeff said. "We can swim later. What do people want to listen to? Lester, how about you?"

Lester stepped out of the doorway and let his arms fly up. "Whooosh!"

"Do you want to hear anything?"

"Supremes," Lester said. He went back in the doorway and pressed his hands against the frame, Samson at the pillars. Maida was suddenly next to me. She had put her arms around my neck and was hugging me, whispering my name. I felt annoyed by the disturbance. I'd just had another thought and lost it when she interrupted.

She rubbed her hand over the back of my shirt. It was my white shirt—I hadn't changed from work—and I wondered what sustained the whiteness, how did the particles of energy hold their whiteness in place? Or was it my mind that thought it white, and the color white was actually a prolonged thought of whiteness?

"Ivan, talk to me, please."

"Why?" I said. My voice sounded far away to me, as though I were speaking through a pipe or into a coffee urn.

"You're so distant."

"I'll be okay," I said.

"I'm not okay. I need you to be more with me."

Jeff came over wearing lipstick and a turban, or maybe his lips just looked red from eating strawberries. But he had wrapped a towel around his head and taken off his shirt. He'd drawn dark circles around his nipples with my leaky pen. I remembered now he'd opened my hand and taken the pen from me and I'd watched my fingers spread out like the speeded-up film of a rose blooming. I looked at my watch. Both hands had stuck together over the two—but that was impossible. We'd already gone past 2:10, unless my watch had stopped, but how could it go backward and stop?

"Sure," Maida said and stood up to dance with Jeff. I'd have to make a note of that: Maida stood up to dance with Jeff *as if he'd asked her*. . . . She put her head on his shoulder. Stop, I thought, and shook my watch. Stop. Stop. Stop. But I meant the opposite. The opposite of that opposite.

Then the room flattened out and I was above it looking down and watching Maida and Jeff kiss. I heard a sound like *Moragggh,* as if the record player had suddenly been unplugged in the middle of a song. But the record was still spinning and Jeff was rubbing Maida's sides, her breasts, and she was squeezing her eyes shut and holding his hips against her, and then I saw myself sitting there watching them and I plunged.

Maida and Jeff were next to me. "What's wrong?"

"What do you mean?"

"You screamed."

"I went up," I said. "I saw you from up there." I pointed to the corner. "I was above you."

Maida rubbed my hands. Jeff put his arm around me. "It's all right," he said. "Take it easy. Think grounded thoughts. Hold onto this." He gave me his toothbrush to hold.

"I don't want to hold your toothbrush! I was up there. Don't you believe me?"

"Ivan," Maida said. "Don't freak out."

"I'm not freaking out." Jeff had gone somewhere. I turned my head and he was gone. "My mind unplugged—my senses, that is. It sounded like the record stopping." I made the sound— *Moragggh*. "But it was my other body slipping out of my physical body. I was up there watching you."

Jeff came back with a glass of water. "Drink this slowly," he said. I dipped my finger in the water and stirred. The water's molecules jumped away from my finger. I held the glass up for Maida. "Do you see that?"

"He's really freaking out," Maida said.

They were talking about me in the third person now, so I did too.

"He wants to know something," I said.

"Don't do this, Ivan. You're scaring me."

"Do you love each other? He wants to know."

Maida looked pained.

I pointed to their eyes. "Do your two you's love your one another's?" The room was starting to spin again, like before, flatten out and be sucked onto the record disc. I could feel a tear, a rip starting in my vision. "I'm going up," I said.

"Let's go outside, all right, buddy?" Jeff said.

"Can he see her breasts?"

"Just take it easy."

"If he can see her breasts he won't go up."

I lifted Maida's shirt. She started to cry, but I had to touch her nipples. They felt warm, thought-less, safe, pink, quiet, and down. The tear closed up.

I had a thought: Lester. Then a gun fired. The thought and the sound happened at the same moment and they were indistinguishable. Only when I saw Jeff run into Lester's room did I know something was wrong.

Lester was lying on his bed, his big body spread across the mattress, his arm over the side, the gun hanging from his finger with the barrel touching the floor. His eyes were wide open, a dead stare up at the ceiling.

"Oh my God," Jeff said and went over to him and began touching Lester all over, looking for the wound.

"Don't do that!" Lester said, giggling. "I'm so ticklish. It drives me crazy!"

I stared at Lester. Jeff backed away from him, then shouted, "You stupid schmuck! This isn't funny!"

Lester sat up on the bed. "I wanted to experience my death."

Jeff sunk to the floor, shaking his head back and forth. "No, no, no, no, *no*, this is all wrong!"

"It was just a blank," Lester said. He emptied the gun and showed us. "I didn't want to hurt anyone." The skin over his face tightened—as though someone were turning a handle on the side of his head. I could see the outline of his skull, what it was going to look like.

I checked behind me. Maida hadn't come into the room. I went back to where she had been sitting and she wasn't there. "Maida?" My voice echoed through the rooms—like the rooms of houses in dreams.

"Ivan, help me," Maida said, and I followed her voice into the bathroom.

She was standing at the sink washing her face.

"What's wrong?"

"I can't see. I keep washing my eyes but I can't see anything."

The chef rushed Maida to the hospital. He had come up to the recreation hall because of the noise. Jeff and I went along, while Lester stayed behind. The chef kept asking me what happened, how did she suddenly go blind? I held Maida's head against my chest and told him I didn't know. Not until we got to the hospital did I admit to the doctor that we had taken acid.

He immediately gave Maida a shot and she fell asleep. He said he was almost positive she would have her sight back in the morning when she woke, but what had happened? How much LSD had we taken? How long ago? And, finally, he asked, Why? That's when I began crying. I had blinded her as surely as if I'd taken a red-hot poker to her eyes. I'd made her do this to prove she loved me. The doctor gave me a Thorazine capsule to bring me down. He said I could stay in Maida's room with her overnight.

The Thorazine helped me but I couldn't fall asleep. I thought I had to make sure Maida was all right, and that by staying awake and watching over her I'd protect her. The chef had gone back to the hotel. I had asked him to wait until morning to tell Letty what had happened. I would call Letty then and take a cab back with Maida. Jeff slept on the couch in the waiting room, half talking to me when I wandered back and forth from there to Maida's room, watching her sleep—her still body, her unseeing eyes, her quiet breathing. I apologized over and over to her. I said I loved her. I bent down to kiss her but Jeff's face superimposed itself over mine as I did, and I withdrew my lips.

Aunt Letty asked us all to leave the hotel after the incident. I remember the shame I felt in facing her, her few but deliberate words: "I think you should go home, Ivan." She would call an agency and find replacements for us. Lester had already gone by the time I returned that next evening. He had left Maida a letter explaining he didn't realize the prank would scare her so much. He also admitted that he wasn't in West Point. He wasn't even in college, or the army. He'd been rejected from the service because of high blood pressure. The uniform belonged to his brother, who was at West Point. He'd signed his letter to Maida, *Sorry,* and enclosed a card for a free pizza.

Maida didn't get out of the hospital that next day, or the next, or the next. It was six weeks before she got her sight back. She had to work with a psychiatrist, who said the incident had been a flashback to her father's death and that her mind had shut down at the sound of the gun. I thought it was true: parts of the mind are so fragile they are thrown into a self-protective darkness at such times, the self hiding from the self.

It was three years before I saw Maida again. The occurrence had caused conflict in our family, and it was generally agreed that it would be a good idea if I didn't contact her. One day she called me at college in Ohio and said that Letty had died.

I was saddened by the news and wanted to fly to New York for the funeral.

I sat in the back of the funeral home while the rabbi talked privately, one by one, with each immediate family member in the front row. I could see Maida's head moving as the rabbi spoke softly to her. She was wearing a simple black dress and her hair was full and long on her back, not in a braid as she had worn it most of that summer. I felt my heart jump when I saw her and I was aware how much I had missed her.

After the funeral we gathered at her mother's house. In all the grief, no one noticed me at first. Then Maida's older sister welcomed me and said how nice it was I could come. Letty had cared a great deal for me, she said. I was thrilled at her words, this forgiveness implied not just from Letty but from her. I had carried around the blame for Maida's blindness for so long I never thought I'd be released from it. "I'm sorry about everything," I said, and Maida's sister squeezed my hand and went over to sit with her mother.

I was standing at the table putting some cheese on a cracker, not because I was hungry but because I felt I should eat. I'd been too nervous on the plane, and now that I was here the excitement had persisted. Maida came up beside me. She took my arm and said to come with her a moment. She was wearing heels and perfume and seemed older than me, as though more time had passed for her.

We went to the backyard and sat on a bench beneath a magnolia tree. When I leaned my head back and looked up, the purple and white blossoms appeared to have the hidden convolutions of conch shells.

Maida held her hands in her lap, formally. There was a distance between us, an affectionate distance, but still a distance. We were cousins now.

"Thanks for calling me," I said.

"I'm glad you came, Ivan."

Her sister shouted from the house. One of Maida's elderly aunts wanted to see her inside.

"In a minute," Maida said.

"Is this hard for you?"

"Yes. Although it's different than his was."

I knew who "his" was without asking. It was the kind of phrasing that made it clear her father's death was never far from her thoughts.

"That was more tense," she said. "Here, people are sad in an accepting way."

"What do you think was behind the tenseness exactly?"

"Bitterness," Maida said. "And I guess this is finally the sweet side of that bitterness. About time. Everybody loved Letty. You always asked me such good questions, Ivan. I really miss you."

I nodded. I was afraid to say much more.

"Are you still going to be a psychologist?"

"Trying," I said.

"I need to tell you something, Ivan. It's about Jeff. We saw each other a few times when he came down to the city."

"I know," I said. "He told me. It was one of the last letters I got from him before he went over."

"I just thought I had to tell you, in case you didn't know. I liked the honesty we had, that's rare I've been finding out. Have you heard from Jeff recently?"

"No."

"I haven't either. It didn't work out, by the way—no surprise, I guess. I think I was attracted to his flamboyance."

"Your father," I said.

Maida smiled at me. "You're such a psychologist."

Maida's elderly aunt came to the door. "Maida, darling! Maida, come here, sweetheart."

"I've got to go, that's Aunt Cissy. She wants to rave about my beautiful hair for a while. It's what she does every time she comes to visit. You'll be okay?"

"Sure," I said. Maida stood up. She took my hand and then kissed me on the cheek. Her hand rested on the back of my neck for a few seconds. I watched her walk over to her aunt and heard the old woman say, "Oh, my God, who has such hair!"

That afternoon I took the train into Manhattan. The sun was bright and the New Yorkers friendly, if I said hello first. I bought a pretzel and got lost on the subway. A black man who sat down next to me wanted to sell me a watch; I said no. He followed me up the steps asking if I needed a toaster, a radio, or a TV. I walked to Central Park and watched a troupe of mimes performing an antiwar skit; "Nixon" stood on his hands and talked the whole time with his feet. It was 1970, and Cambodia had just been invaded. In a month I would hear that Jeff was killed in Vietnam when his jeep rode over a land mine. It seemed that for being so young I'd loved a lot of people who had died.

I didn't know what to do with myself for the rest of the day. I'd told Maida I had some friends to see in New York, but I'd actually come only to attend the funeral and to see her. There was nowhere else to go now but home.

Navajo Cafe

They had left the Grand Canyon early in the morning and driven onto the Navajo Indian reservation in search of a Navajo taco. A friend of Charles's had urged him to make sure he stopped out West for a Navajo taco: a large wheel of fried dough, like a popover, smothered in beans, green chilies, lettuce, tomatoes, and cheese. Except that Devra, Charles's ten-year-old daughter, refused to touch her smaller child's portion, now that it had finally arrived. She said it looked like a cowpie. It did look like a cowpie, Charles agreed, only a good cowpie. Still, she'd gone into a sulk, stubbornly refusing to eat or even talk to him.

She had grown increasingly pouty and uncooperative on the trip. Last year's vacation had been so easy that he should have known not to expect the same results this year. But he thought she would be old enough for a cross-country trip (they lived in Connecticut) to see the West: the Grand Canyon, the Painted Desert, Monument Valley, Yellowstone, the Rockies, Carlsbad Caverns . . . Stuckey's. They'd planned a burro ride into the Grand Canyon, down the Bright Angel trail. At the last moment Devra became frightened and wouldn't stay on her mule, kicking at the indifferent animal, who was evidently used to temperamental children and just continued urinating without pause. Finally, Charles had to lift her off; they were holding up the mule train. He settled for a cup of hot chocolate and an "I Hiked the Canyon" T-shirt in the visitors' lodge.

She had been hysterical like this once before, two years ago, when the sock incident happened. It was the anniversary of her mother's death. Charles had been walking by Devra's bedroom when he overheard her say to her friend CeeCee, who was spending the night, "I'll trade you one divorcée and one old maid for a widower and an adulteress." Her friend had asked, "What's the adult dress look like?"

Where did she learn these things? Charles had wondered. He carefully supervised her TV watching. He could understand the widower—Charles had been referred to as that—but the divorcée, the adulteress? "Deal," CeeCee agreed, and then there was so much squealing and giggling and howling that he opened the door to see what was going on. They'd stuffed socks with toilet paper and put rubber bands around the toes to make heads. About thirty sock dolls were on either side of the bed. In the middle was a Dutch oven filled with steaming water. One drenched sock doll tied to a stick was being dunked in the water. "What are you doing?" Charles asked, more incredulous than angry. But they took his tone for a scolding and both burst into tears, cowering together in the corner as if they'd committed the most shameful act possible. "You didn't knock, Daddy! You didn't knock first!" Devra screamed out through her tears, shaking all over, this one pitiful comment her only defense against a torturous punishment she seemed to believe would result from the evil deed. Her little friend was so frightened she began hicupping, choking on her tears. "It's okay," Charles reassured them, "it's all right to play. Go back to playing. I was just wondering if you wanted some popcorn. I didn't mean to barge in," and he left the room quickly.

Downstairs, the image of all those puff-headed sock dolls, with wadded up toilet paper and rubber bands twisted around their necks, stayed with him. He put some oil in a pan for popcorn. Suddenly CeeCee ran down the stairs, grabbed the front doorknob with both hands, and dashed out before he could catch her. Charles went back upstairs, as nonthreatening as he could make himself, picking up a plant from the hallway so it would look as though he were on his way to water it. He knocked on her door. No answer. He opened it and came in with the fern. She was already in bed with her pajamas on, the light turned off. Two hours before her bedtime, it was only 7:30. She kept her face pressed into the pillow, still trembling, and pretending to be asleep in the midst of her violent shivering. He stroked her hair, which had always calmed her before but now only made her dig her face harder into the pillow, filling him with pity and sadness and a terrible helplessness at not knowing what to do. He sat with her for an hour. Even after she was asleep he had to unclench her fingers from his pant leg. On the way out, he picked up one of the sock dolls.

He examined it carefully, unable to see why she had been so terrified at being caught; it wasn't the first time she'd been a little mischievous . . . a couple of rolls of toilet paper gone, but no big deal. Then he suddenly saw that these weren't the socks he washed every week at all; these were Amanda's socks, her mother's. Devra had taken them from one of the trunks Charles had packed after the accident. She'd opened the trunk . . . and made puppets from her dead mother's socks, meaning to punish and drown them in hot water. No wonder the poor child was frightened. Caught playing a harmless game, in her mind she must have connected it with all sorts of horrible malevolence. Charles went back upstairs and sat by her bed so he'd be there if she woke up, wondering if the game were some unconscious anger Devra needed to express against her mother for abandoning her.

"I heard a story about a little boy who also wouldn't eat his food," Charles told her now, trying to get her to take a bite. Devra was watching some Indian children at a table on the other side of the cafe. They were sipping Cokes and eating hamburgers. In fact, he saw no one else eating Navajo tacos. An old Navajo woman came in wearing a squashblossom necklace against a blue velveteen blouse, and long, flowing skirts. "That's a traditional Indian outfit," Charles pointed out to Devra. A Navajo man in the booth ahead glanced around at Charles. He looked young, educated. Charles thought perhaps his remark had been patronizing, but he didn't see any harm in identifying the way a different culture dressed. It wasn't as though everyone in here looked the same. Their waitress, for instance, appeared a typical enough American teenager—her hair layered fashion-ably on the sides, and she wore a gold chain instead of Indian jewelry around her neck.

"There's this little boy named Stanley," explained Charles, hoping the story would distract her enough to eat. "Stanley is five years old and has never said *a single word.*" Devra, in spite of herself, turned toward him with interest. "One day he's sitting at the breakfast table and he says out of the clear blue, 'The oatmeal is lumpy.' His parents are very very happy. 'Stanley,' his mom says, 'you spoke, darling! Your first words! We're so pleased!' After the excitement dies down a little, Dad leans over and asks, 'How did this happen, son? I mean, you haven't spoken *a word* for five years and suddenly you talk. Not that we're finding fault, but why is that, son?' And Stanley looks at them with a very serious face and says, 'Up until now things have been just fine.'"

Devra stared at him.

"Well, *I* thought it was funny," said Charles, not knowing whether she didn't get it or she just had better taste than he did. "Okay, Miss Silent Puss, I think we'll call it a day since you insist on being such bad company. I'm not going to waste my breath trying to get you to eat—or talk. You have no reason to behave this way."

"I do, too."

Her first words in an hour. "And what is that?"

She didn't answer him. She continued sitting with folded arms. Her hair was too long and he wished she'd agree to have it cut. One day some demonic meatball would yank it back on the playground and she'd be in a wheelchair the rest of her life. She was small and thin for her age, with green eyes that could be impenetrable or determined, as they were now, or so glassy and ethereal that he worried where her mind went. She was at a stage where she wouldn't let herself be seen undressed, or wear shorts unless she had leotards underneath. When he asked her why not—she had such cute legs—she broke into tears and said they were ugly green celery sticks and not part of this world.

They belonged to Udau, a mythical playmate she used to blame everything on, whom she hadn't mentioned in years.

He asked the waitress for the check. "She had a big breakfast," Charles said, excusing Devra's untouched meal. "You don't have to wrap it," he added, although the girl hadn't given any indication of doing so. While she went to make change, the Indian in the booth in front, who had glanced at him, stood up and stretched. He wore a leather vest over a faded pink union shirt, wraparound sunglasses, and on his wrist a heavy silver bracelet embedded with a fat piece of turquoise. He kept nodding at Charles. It was peculiar. None of the other Indians gave him a second look, while this one seemed ready to dance with him. Finally Charles felt uncomfortable enough to say something. "Excuse me, do you know how far we are from Flagstaff?" The Indian just stared at him uncomprehendingly, rolling his shoulders back. His neck was muscular and loose, cracking freely. Charles listened to the bones popping, the Indian sucking air through his teeth—his thumbs hooked at the waist around empty belt loops. "Flagstaff, Arizona?" Charles repeated. Maybe he didn't understand English. Or was slow. Or on drugs.

The Indian came over to their table. He squatted down so his chin was even with the edge. He took off his sunglasses, looked deeply at Charles, then at Devra, then back at Charles, and then sang in a warbling voice:

"I got those walking talking crying Yiddish blues. Oh, baby, ain't I so low. I got me backaches and sideaches and bellyaches and heartaches. I got me the way way way way down walking talking crying Yiddish blues. I got the meanest old mean, I got the hurtest old hurt, I got the troublest old trouble, I got me those walking talking crying Yiddish blues."

"Jesus!" said Charles.

The Indian stood up, clasped his hands behind his neck, yawned, stretched, sucked air, and then, without turning his head, pointed a stiff finger over his shoulder. "Flagstaff, that way," he said, and ambled out the door. Charles looked around the restaurant. The other Indians were ignoring them. The waitress was leaning over the counter, eating a piece of custard pie. She'd forgotten his change.

"Oh, Lord!" Charles said. Devra sat impassively, unaffected by the performance. "Didn't you see what happened? That was an *Indian!*"

"Don't notice me," said Devra, and slumped farther down in her seat.

They drove on a two-lane road that cut across the northern part of the reservation. Crazy Indians. Really strange. Devra sat in the back reading a book. He would let her be moody today. Tomorrow, right away, he'd put his foot down and make it clear they weren't having any more of this nonsense . . . or they were going home. He suspected much of her behavior was because he'd asked her in a roundabout way what she would think of his remarrying. One morning at breakfast he'd hinted, "Would you like to see more of Peg around the house?" He regularly spent two nights a week with Peg, always feeling a little guilty when he dropped Devra off for the evening at her grandmother's. "Where?" Devra had answered cagily, lifting her eyes toward the bedroom. "Just around the house," said Charles, unable to bring himself to be more definite. Devra had shrugged, making him feel ashamed and uncomfortable, as if his desires were unfair to her. He somehow needed the approval of this ten year old for all his actions. A therapist he had been seeing, a woman in her sixties, asked him why he felt this way when he brought up the subject later.

"Because I feel guilty?"

"Do you?"

"I wasn't even there. It was a plane crash. I had no control over it."

"Control," the therapist repeated.

"But I didn't."

"Then that must not be it."

"Maybe I want to be sure she likes me."

"Are you afraid she doesn't?"

"No, I know she does. I'm her father. She has to like me."

"Oh, come now, Mr. Timmerman. That's never stopped children before."

The woman could be brutally observant. "I mean, she doesn't have a choice."

"Oh?"

"Choice in a different way."

"You mean she doesn't have a mother. You're her *only* choice."

"Right. I have to be both to her."

"Impossible, Mr. Timmerman. You're only one person. And if you continue trying to be two, you'll continue to be disappointed and indecisive, as you are now. You can take responsibility for your own actions, but not for those of someone who isn't alive."

Charles had squeezed the rubber jacks ball he'd gotten in the habit of holding during the sessions.

"Control, Mr. Timmerman. Control is not your life's work."

It was getting dark and they were almost clear of the reservation. He'd pointed out what sights there were to Devra—the octagonal houses of logs and mud that were called hogans, the mesas, the sheep grazing near the road, but she'd kept her nose in the book. He felt invigorated by the open country, the expanse of earth, the hard, red rock and quiet authority of the land, the yucca plants with their white stalks full of blossoms shooting into the clear sky, while everything else seemed to hug the ground—a terrain that favored views from the belly, the hogans popping up occasionally like loaves of round bread.

He glanced in the mirror at her now and thought that things might be all right. He had nothing more to go on than the excitement brought about by the drive—the possibilities in this unwalled land—that he could give her a comfortable life, no, more than that: a hopeful one. He knew he could be a good father and that she loved him and that he would never stop worrying about her. He would always struggle with himself against trying to reach inside and fix her view of the world, a view that wheedled against despair, that countered all losses, and that tried to insure an impossible equity. Probably what she needed, even as a ten year old, was for him to stop fussing over her, to take a breath free of his inspection, to fail on her own without feeling as though nothing else could go wrong because something too terrible had already happened. He had to admit, though, that if he worried about dying and leaving her alone in the world, his greatest fear was that *he* had no one else. He had made it through the worst parts of her mother's death by thinking, with a cold assurance that made him wince now, there's still Devra left. A day hadn't passed when he hadn't bargained that they can take anyone, but not her, a feeling that had started the moment he touched her and held her weight in his arms, her presence a vivid connection for him to a self deeper than any other . . . not from his mind, but from his heart to her baby's heart.

"Are you hungry, Dev?" The calmness in his voice made her speak up unguarded and say yes. He turned around and was about to say they would stop for dinner—no more Navajo tacos—when there was a dull thud and she screamed "You hit him! You hit him!" Her scream continued as Charles, moaning reflexively, pulled the car off the road.

He unfastened his seat belt and told Devra to wait in the car, but she screamed so desperately that he took her in hand and went running down the road, terrified of what he would see, the low moan still rolling in his throat, a sudden shame that his bowels might erupt—his fear was this penetrating. He squeezed her hand.

An old man was sitting up beneath an embankment where he'd evidently tumbled after being hit. "Are you hurt?" Charles asked. The old man was an Indian, his face deeply wrinkled in the dim light of a bar back from the road. He reeked of liquor. "Didn't you see me?"

"He doesn't speak English," said an Indian woman who had come up from the parking lot. Her friend had gone inside to call an ambulance.

"I didn't even see him coming. Where was he?"

"Over there," she said, and pointed across the road. "He sits over there when he drinks too much."

"Did you see him cross?"

The Indian woman hesitated. "No."

Charles couldn't believe this was the same man he'd hit. Sixty miles an hour. He remembered glancing at the speedometer before looking back at Devra. The man should be dead.

"I saw the whole thing," a truck driver said, running over and out of breath. He had pulled his rig into the parking lot of the bar. He was white. He leaned over and shouted in the old man's ear. "Your leg hurt, grandpa? Can you stand up?"

"Maybe he shouldn't—"

"That's it. Lean on my shoulder." Once up, the old man wobbled unsteadily, although it could have been from being drunk. The truck driver helped him sit down again, and the old man went back to rubbing his leg.

"His leg?" Charles asked.

"I think he's all right."

"I was going so fast. I don't understand why he's—"

"These guys are loose as a goose when they're drunk like this. He rolled with the punch. Must have been like being hit by a big plunger."

"But anybody would be . . . should be . . . "

"Look, don't argue with luck. You hit the loosest, highest old Indian around."

Charles bent down and held Devra. Both of them were shivering. The desert air chilled quickly at night, and he was trembling anyway, now that it was starting to sink in, how lucky they'd all been. They stood silently around the old man and waited for the ambulance to arrive. Charles desperately needed a drink from the bar, but he didn't want alcohol on his breath. Trucks flew by on the highway, sucking them in their draft.

A siren came from the distance, then a police car pulled up. "Listen," the truck driver said. "Don't let these guys push you around. They've got no authority over white people."

"Who are they?" Charles asked.

"Navajo police. You're right on the border here, so it's still their jurisdiction, sort of."

The Navajo cop came over. He was a short man with straight black hair that lay flat over his forehead. He said something in Navajo to the old man. They carried on a conversation for a while, and finally Charles couldn't stand his own silence and said he'd been driving the car. The cop looked at him, then stated in a voice without accusation, "He says you didn't have your lights on."

"Yes, he did," the truck driver put in before Charles could answer. "I saw the whole thing. Grandpa here walked right in front of him."

The Navajo cop didn't say anything. Charles kept silent, too. He actually had no idea what had happened, except he was sure his lights were on. Then he'd looked back at Devra, and thump . . . not the sound of glass shattering or metal denting or stone crumbling or even rubber bouncing, as the truck driver imagined, but of flesh thumping, an unnatural sound . . . a simple, muffled, almost polite noise.

An ambulance arrived in tandem with a state police car. The state cop, a young, reedy kid with a Western twang, immediately came over and asked what had happened. Charles explained, and the cop kept nodding in such a way that Charles knew the kid had made up his mind about any accident involving an Indian even before he got here. The truck driver repeated his version of the story, how the old man walked dead drunk right in front of Charles's car. The Navajo cop listened but didn't interfere. "Let's look at your car," the state cop said. Charles asked the truck driver to watch Devra; he didn't want her walking down the dark highway unnecessarily. She sat down alongside the old man, who was being examined by the ambulance crew.

The cop shined his flashlight on Charles's Connecticut license plate, wrote down the numbers, then went around front. He didn't ask to see Charles's driver's license. "There you go," he said, pointing to a small crack fanning out like a seashell on the passenger's side of the windshield. "You must have got him when you swerved."

"What do you mean?"

"I don't see how he could crack your windshield here unless you swerved."

Charles didn't answer. The other possibility, he knew, was that the old man was already past the car—not stepping in front of it, as the truck driver claimed, but grazed by the car as Charles sped by.

Walking back, the state cop told him these accidents happen all the time. They were on the line, just across the border of the reservation. Liquor wasn't allowed on the reservation, so bars were built at every entrance and Indians came out here and got drunk and then killed themselves on the way home along the dark highways. This was the third pedestrian-auto accident this month; the other two hadn't been so lucky. "How fast were you going?" the cop asked. Charles tensed up. "About sixty," he said. The cop shook his head. "One acrobatic Indian."

"Do you have to make a report?"

"Not unless you want it for the insurance company."

"Insurance company?"

"Your windshield."

"No," Charles said. He just wanted to get out of here as fast as possible. "Is there a motel nearby?"

"About ten miles ahead."

He thanked the cop and then said goodbye to the truck driver, thanking him also for stopping. The old man still sat against the embankment, next to Devra. He had been saying something to her as Charles walked up.

The Navajo cop helped the old man into the police car; he would take him home. Not a word had been exchanged between the two police. "He'll be all right, won't he?" Charles asked. No one answered him. Only Devra and he were left. Everyone else had left as quickly as they had appeared. Charles suddenly regretted not apologizing to the old man, but he'd been too worried about fault and blame to do what seemed decent and natural.

Devra rode up front with him. He was glad to see she understood how he felt. He couldn't take her acting up now. His back was tense as steel, his legs locked; he forced himself to shift the car into gear, then slowly pull onto the road. Gradually he increased his speed until he was confident enough to do what felt like a reckless forty miles per hour. A truck bore down from behind. He hugged the right side of the road until the double trailer passed.

"I saw that old man say something to you."

"Yes," Devra said.

Charles laughed. "He must have thought you were an Indian."

Devra was silent.

"He did speak Navajo to you, right?"

"Didn't."

Charles shifted his eyes, not turning his head from the road, but trying to see her expression. "Come on, Dev, he couldn't speak a word of English."

"He could. If he wanted."

"All right. What did he tell you?"

"Lots of stuff."

"Like what?"

"Just stuff." Devra moved in her seat. "He told me not to tell most of it."

"That's fine. You should keep secrets."

"You don't believe me."

Charles considered a moment. "No, I suppose I can't. Not this time."

"He said you wouldn't."

"Fine," Charles said, wanting to let the subject drop and not appreciating when she played fancifully with the truth, perhaps having heard the old man say words and then just supplying her own interpretation. He sometimes sensed that she might tease men when she grew older, learn the fine art of deceit— with all its attendant self-mystery.

"I could tell you one thing."

"If you want."

"He asked me if I was scared."

"Did he?"

"He said not to be. I wasn't supposed to be scared. It was a mistake and I could stop. My being afraid."

"And what are you afraid of?"

"Everything."

"There must be *something* you're not afraid of?"

"No," Devra said with certainty.

Charles reached for her hand. "Are you going to listen to this old man then and stop?"

"Yes."

"Well, I'm glad for that."

She fell asleep before they reached the motel. After he registered and put her to bed, he went outside to get ice. But the machine was broken, so he returned to the room and sat on his bed, spread out the *Navajo Times,* and rubbed his feet through his socks. He watched her sleep with the pillow pulled tight around her ears like a bonnet, a new pose, probably a superstitious one. She'd once spent a week refusing to bathe, wearing a necklace of Puffed Wheat that supposedly belonged to Gulada the Taradiddle Queen. The funny thing was that he could watch her all night. Stare at a sleeping child with a pillow over her head. That's all it was. A child at rest. Reduced respiration. Accelerated gamma waves. Temperature decline. Held limbs. He wouldn't do it, though. He wouldn't watch her. They both needed to rest.

Down Under

My uncle is a landlord in Philadelphia and I am his assistant. When customers descend the steps into his basement office, he jumps to his feet, rocks back on his heels, listens patiently while they request a safe apartment with a front view, spits a piece of cigar over a trash can stuffed with bills, and then asks, "Students?" If they answer yes, he says, that's good, because I only rent to students. If they answer no, he only says, that's good. Then he digs into one of the cigar boxes stacked precariously on his desk, emptying keys from little brown envelopes into his palm. After staring at them thoughtfully, he slides the keys back into their envelopes and starts the process over again with other packets. When he's gone through every box, cursing his workers for not returning the keys, he will slash the mound of utility bills, citations, repair lists, payments, leases, screwdrivers, nails, and styrofoam cups, scrape together a fistful of keys, drop them into my hands, and discharge me into the street on my mission.

I've promised my father that I will help Uncle Sid for the summer while I'm home from college, and now I wait in the office for him to return. Willie and Oliver are in their places. Willie slumps in the old easy chair that swallows him up like a pickle barrel. Oliver sits hunched over on the wooden stool in the corner. Because Sid's checkbook has been stolen once, and because whenever it slips behind his desk he accuses one of these men of stealing it, I have to stand guard in the suffocating basement room. The men, on the other hand, choose to wait here, believing the closer they are to Sid's checkbook, the better chance they have of getting their money.

"Where your uncle at?" Willie asks me. "He don't come back here soon, you gonna have to forge them checks. Or pay us the nickel outa you own pocket."

Oliver laughs so hard at this that he has one of his coughing spells and must beat his thighs to stop. Oliver could be forty or sixty. I don't know, and neither does anyone else. His eyes are always puffy and bloodshot, he coughs continually, and he's so thin and frail that he can barely hold a paintbrush steady, the only job he's able to do anymore. He's worked for Sid twenty years, as has Willie, who handles most of the repairs, only a fraction of which actually get fixed. Willie's leg is laced with pins, and he limps to work with a cane and a thermos of whiskey under his arm. And Sid himself is a picture of poor health, with high blood pressure and two heart attacks on his record.

I hear Sid on the stairs, puffing and grunting even though he's going down. He shuffles in wearing a heavy brown suit in this heat, his face flushed, his collar pinching the roll of fat at the back of his neck. Only his hair is combed neatly, wavy, blond, almost golden: the ladykiller of the family, as he was once called—forty years younger and a hundred pounds lighter. Now he seems stuffed into his polyester suit, his arteries ready to rip. Because of Sid's heart condition, my father has asked me to lend a hand to his only brother during the heat of the summer. In return Sid will give me money for school. But what was supposed to be a temporary job has turned into a full-time preoccupation. At night I lie awake worrying about the leaking roofs, the rats, the fire code violations, the eviction notices, the security deposits not given back, the slave wages he pays his help.

Sid's eyes fall first on Oliver, sitting farthest away on the wooden stool, who with pursed lips and artistic care is turning the pages of the *Daily News*.

"You finish at the Sutton?"

"I run outa paint."

"The almond?"

Oliver doesn't look up. He wets his finger to turn a page. "Uh-huh."

"You know Gene has ten cans of it downstairs."

"I don' know that."

"Go back there and finish the living room. Mark will run you down."

"It's five o'clock!"

"It's a quarter till and you didn't get here until eleven today." Sid stares down at his desk, remembering. "And, Willie, you go with him. Somebody's missing a door down there, B-8, yeah, it's B-8."

"I ain't fixing no door! I'm going home and rest this leg 'fore I have to sell it to you as a busted pipe!"

"Fix the door. Just get it back on the hinges. You can put the molding on tomorrow."

"Molding? Where the molding gone? I ain't fixing no door. It's quittin' time."

"Fix the door."

"Give me my check first."

"After you fix the door."

"I ain't hobblin' all the way back here to pick up no check!"

"Just fix the damn door!"

"My check!"

"Get out!"

"Don't get hot—"

"Don't tell me what to do!"

"I ain't telling you nothing. I just want my money so's I don't have to come back."

I close my eyes and retreat farther back against the wall, dreaming of fresh air. I listen to the voices, Sid's raw threats, hollow from years of suspicion and abuse; Willie's empty bark that always ends in a cowering whine, trying to save face while it pleads; my father's instructions not to let Sid climb any stairs. I hear the tenants screaming out operatic complaints, their windows banging shut on the steel backs of roaches. I hear the police rapping on doors, evicting in harmony. And I hear my own voice, perfectly pitched, blending in a gospel of frustration and discontent.

"Sid," I say, "it's five o'clock. Let me hold Willie's check. I'll take him down."

Sid stares at me, not recognizing a safe voice, perhaps sensing by now that I am not clearly on his side and would give Willie his check once we were outside.

"I can hold my own damn check!" says Willie, who is too stubborn and proud in his unending battle with Sid to let me help him.

I look around the office: pole lamps on their sides, too tall for anywhere but the Sistine Chapel; a Budweiser clock stuck at 6:30; a bowl of wax fruit melted into a mutant purple lump; a coffee table with sawed-off legs; a mattress with yellow stains leaning against the wall; lampshades with yellow burns in the corner; plumbing fixtures corroded beyond recognition on the filing cabinet; bedrails layered with rust; a shoebox full of jammed locks and twisted keys; a decade of ragged telephone books stacked on a broken air conditioner that occupies the only window in the office. Nothing is discarded unless it hops in a trash can and finds its way up the stairs.

"Get out of here," Sid says, pushing Willie toward the door, finally handing him his check. "You, too, Oliver." He gives Oliver a few dollars and some change for the bus. Then he turns to me. "You need anything?"

"I'm fine."

"Got enough gas in the car?"

"It's okay."

"You want some club soda for the ride?"

"Really, I'm fine."

He gives me two quick pats on the back, then transfers some rent money from his pocket to an envelope. I feel the envelope sink in my hand. For a moment I just hold it in front of me, remembering Sid shaking Oliver so hard this afternoon that Oliver threw up (he lost another apartment key). Finally I take the money. "Tomorrow at eight, then," Sid says, once I do.

*   *   *

After a restless night, I leave early in the morning, drive into Philadelphia as I have for the past three months, and wait outside Sid's office for the workers.

"Mark," says my uncle, leaning into the car, "this is Warren. Let him finish painting number six on Lombard. After you drop him off, take Willie around to the Sutton."

I've never seen Warren before. He hunches over in the back seat, his breath heavy with liquor. That, in addition to something malevolent about him, a conspicuous scar on his neck, an indifferent nod at me, a scowl on his face that shifts itself through stages of disgust, and the dress pants and silk shirt he's wearing make me wonder why Sid let him work.

Once we're moving, Willie says, "You hear 'bout Gene shooting his wife?"

"Gene our manager?" I'm stunned by this news. Gene is one of the gentlest men I know.

"Shot her through the hand last night. He's in jail right now."

"He really shot her?" It becomes harder to believe the more I think about it. "Why?"

"Yeah, it was hot last night." Willie reaches into his toolbox for his thermos. He takes a drink, then passes it back to Warren. "Them people don't get some water soon, they gonna deep-fry your uncle."

"Since when don't they have water?"

"Since yesterday when I shut it down trying to fix them leaks. The piping ain't no good."

I lean over the steering wheel, thinking about the Sutton Arms, Sid's all-black apartment building, 75 units, that has been condemned twice and remains operating by borderline repairs. "They'll tear the place down if they don't have water by tonight."

"They probably tear you up as it is just for being Sid's nephew. Ain't that right, Warren?" I glance in the mirror at Warren. He blinks his eyes shut to answer. "You can't really blame ol' Gene. The trouble started when the men come home from work and don't find no water—again. They bang on Gene's door. He tell them he think it be fixed tomorrow. They say they gonna kill him if he don't do something right now. So he sit behind his door the whole night, a bottle in one hand, a gun in the other. The men keep banging and finally say they coming in after him. So Gene panic and tell them, 'I give you Sidney's nephew you leave me be!'"

"Oh, come on—so he didn't shoot her then?"

"Sure he shoot her, boy! He got to show them he serious 'bout turning you over, don't he? How else you gonna convince crazy people 'cept by shooting your own wife?"

I give up trying to find out the truth. After we drop Warren off, I park in front of the Sutton. The sidewalk is unswept. Orange peels and Dunkin Donut wrappers fill the mailboxes. In the lobby ceiling is a huge gash and sticking up through it on a ladder is Oliver.

"How's it going, Oliver?" I ask him.

"Fine, jus' fine."

"What are you doing up there?"

"Looking, jus' looking."

Willie stops tickling a woman who's trying to wipe her neck with a handkerchief. He grabs me by the arm. "Look at that, boy. See all that patching? That ain't no good. He need a whole new system."

"He can't afford it."

"Well, he gonna *have* to afford it, 'less he planning to dig a well in here."

"Are you positive?"

"The drainage ain't bad but he got to do something quick 'bout them first-floor supply pipes."

"Did you tell him this?"

"There you go being stupid again."

"Then I'll drive back and tell him until he listens."

"Now hold on . . . wait just a second." Willie reaches down for his thermos. "Don't go getting yourself all heated up. I'll take care what I can today, then come Monday maybe I can do something else—"

"Christ, Willie."

"What's wrong?" He stumbles close to my ear. "Talk to your uncle! Talk to the man! See what he say. If he give me the okay,

I come down and put everything in—piping, unions, valves, elbows, everything!"

I trudge upstairs, four flights, blaming Willie, blaming my uncle, blaming myself for coming between fingers pointing to thin air. I unlock the door of a vacant apartment. Near the back of the room, shifting her weight from one leg to the other, Esther pulls dirt from a mop.

"How's everything, Esther?"

"I can't be finishing my work in here if I gotta stop every two minutes to pick away at this here mop!"

I like Esther and do anything I can for her. She takes pride in her work, assigning her own standard of perfection to each apartment she cleans based on its potential condition. If she isn't satisfied with a job, she'll stay until she is, regardless of how many cleanings Sid has scheduled her to do. At the end of the day, she folds her check without even a glance and drops it in her handbag.

"He gonna have to get me a new mop." Esther bangs the handle on the floor. "This one ain't fit to wipe anybody's backside! Just look at that floor."

It seems immaculate to me. "Like a palace ballroom, Esther."

"Oh go on 'bout your business and let me finish in here."

"Sid wants me to bring you over to Fifty-second Street to clean an apartment there."

"I still got the kitchen sink to go in here."

"That won't take long, will it?"

"Shouldn't."

"About ten minutes, then?"

"Wait a second now—ain't Fifty-second Street full up?"

"The new tenants are already in, but it hasn't been cleaned from the old ones yet."

"They there now?"

"I suppose so, why?"

"They men?"

"I think so—why?"

"You gonna be there?"

"No, I have to go . . . why do you want to know all this?"

"I ain't going then."

"What do you mean?"

"I don't clean no apartments when they's occupied or just been occupied."

"For heaven's sake, Esther, why not? Are you in the union or something?"

"I know I'm fat and I know I'm old but that don't make no difference from what all I read in the papers and what I seen with my own eyes."

"Don't be ridiculous, Esther. These guys are students."

"That don't mean a damn thing to me. I don't trust my kind and I don't trust your kind any more."

"These guys aren't going to rape you."

"When I comes to an apartment it's by myself and I stays by myself. I keeps the door locked and I does my work. That's the only way I can *do* my work."

I tap the two keys together. "I think they're med students even."

"I don't care if it the pope and the president playing checkers! I ain't going in there by myself! Your uncle know I don't do apartments like that." Esther curls her lip and picks harder at the mop. "You live down here as long as I do, you know a woman got to be careful 'bout where she go." She reaches into her supply bucket and then points a can of Comet at me. "I seen what happen with people who ain't!"

Esther walks into the kitchen. I sigh heavily and lock the door behind me, slipping the two keys back into their envelope. Downstairs, Oliver is sitting on the bottom step, turning the pages of the *Daily News* with his usual artistry.

"Oliver, I thought I told you to start painting B-10."

"There people in it."

"It's supposed to be vacant."

"S'pose to be."

"Who are they?"

He turns a page. "I don' know."

"Then let's go up and find out, all right?"

"Hey, boy!" Willie's voice booms down through the ceiling. "You just stay put 'less you want to get your head blown off."

"*What* is going on here?"

Willie points his wrench at me. "We already called your uncle and he sending the police down. You sit there and wait for them."

The police arrive an hour later and quietly place the couple in the back seat of a squad car, the girl looking slightly older than the boy, both of them no more than eighteen. There's no damage to the apartment; in fact, the floor has been swept and the stuck window is now working freely. In the farthest corner from the door are a sleeping bag and a candle melted in an ashtray. A cassette recorder on the windowsill is turned up full volume. One policeman gathers the articles while the other points his pencil at me and asks questions. Did I ever see them before? Are there any other vacant apartments? No, I've never seen them before, and yes, there are lots of vacant apartments. They inform me police locks are the best on the market. I explain that we change the locks so often that no one can keep track of the keys. Oliver loses keys all the time. And Esther won't clean an apartment unless there's a deadbolt. Crazy, huh? They stare at me blankly. They don't know Oliver. And they don't care if Esther wraps herself in chains at night. Why am I rambling on? I tell them to see my uncle if they have more questions.

After I've checked the rest of the building, I go downstairs where Oliver, Esther, and Willie are lined up waiting to depart, already time to quit. We load up the car and drive crosstown to pick up Warren, the griddled streets heating up the rush-hour traffic trying to uncoil its way out of the city. Warren is standing outside, taking long gulps from a bottle in a paper bag. I get out of the car to help him put his supplies in and I notice the paint cans all feel full. I glance in the window. One wall has barely been touched; the others are still unpainted.

"What happened, Warren?"

"What d'ya mean 'What happened?'"

"The apartment—you didn't paint it."

"Sure I did! Look at that back wall."

"That's nothing for all the time you've been here."

"C'mon, man, get on."

"I'm serious, Warren. You didn't do a damn thing here."

He presses his lips together, finally bursting out, "Fuck, boy! Who you anyways?"

"I don't see how you expect to get paid for this job."

"You paying me or Sid paying me?"

"He's not going to pay you."

"Let's go talk with the man."

"Why bother? Why should you get paid for a job you didn't do?" He takes a step toward me, squeezing the neck of the bottle.

"Get over here, boy!" Willie shouts at me from the car. I sit down on the steps and fold my arms over my knees. Warren looms above me.

"I'm not taking you back to Sid's, Warren."

"The hell you ain't!"

"I'll take the supplies back. If you want to see him, you can walk. You'll get there just as fast with the traffic."

Warren points the bottle at me. "Sid letting *you* run the business? You ain't got the sense of a fucking little kid!"

I put my head down. "I'm only helping him for the summer— and don't point at me. People have been pointing things at me all day and I'm sick of it."

"What the hell . . . who the hell you then?" He throws the bottle down at my feet. Liquor spills over my shoes. "You ain't nothing! You ain't nothing!" I lean back stiffly against the steps, my whole body tense.

"Get in this car, boy!" Willie yells, kicking open the car door and running between us. "Go on, Warren, meet us 'round Sid's."

Silence, incriminating silence. I drive slowly, ignoring the bourbon on my shoes, sifting the argument of all personal fault.

"Well, do you think I was wrong?" We pull up to a stoplight. More silence. "Well, was I?"

"Just let your uncle take care of it," Willie says.

"Yes or no? Was I wrong in what I said?"

"You wrong *any*time you tell a man he ain't getting paid."

"But he didn't do anything."

"That don't make no difference. You don't put a man at a job and then tell him he ain't getting shit. You at least gonna pay for the mistake of hiring him. Your uncle know what to do. He'll buy the job from him. If it ain't worth nothing, he'll give him close to nothing."

"Sid isn't even here! How's he going to know what happened?"

"You was gonna tell him, right? What you think you doing down here with us—sightseeing?"

"*Jesus,* what do you think I am, a spy?"

"And you got a lot to learn 'bout treating people 'round here," Esther says. "We got a whole way of acting that diff'rent from the folks you used to."

"You don't tell a man like that you keeping his money from him," says Willie.

"Specially when he drunk like he is."

"If I hadn't grabbed you, he mighta slit you so bad you wouldn't know which way your ass was running."

"That man a *goat*," Oliver puts in.

Esther hitches up her shoulders. "We got us a whole lot of nice people in this neighborhood and we got a whole lot of bad ones. And there a diff'rent way of talking with each of them." She nods her head.

"Besides," Willie says, "you don't know what kinda problems that man have. Maybe he got something tore up so bad in him he *cain't* work."

I squint at the road. We're in a long line of traffic. Another column blocks the intersection we need to cross. We wait behind a bus, tasting its acrid fumes, waiting for a space to open. Horns blare violently for something to move. I feel the heat closing in on me, forcing the air out. Oliver hacking at the air in the back. The bourbon burning up the air. The bus choking off the air. I close my eyes. Sid's buildings crumble. The dust catches in my throat. Deep deep, I have to breathe down deep just once—

"Niggers! You're all a bunch of lazy niggers!"

I expect a commotion, a belligerent swearing, an angry muttering, at the very least a hostile silence, but instead they roar with amusement:

"My Lawd! How'd a nigger get in this car!"

"Which of us niggers you talking 'bout, boy?"

"Sid gonna give you a whuppin' he hear you talk like that!"

They hoot and slap me on the back until we pull into the alley alongside Sid's. I jam the car into park, embarrassed and furious over their reaction, needing more than ever to fill my lungs. We all rush inside just ahead of Warren, who is charging around the corner, everyone screaming at once.

"Give me my money!"

"Don't give it to him, Sid!"

"Quiet, boy! What I tell you in the car!"

"He didn't do anything, Sid—"

"I'm gonna punch his head!"

"He didn't do a damn thing!"

"SHUT UP! I SAYS SHUT UP!" In the corner, grinning and pleased with himself, Oliver uncups his hands from his mouth.

"What happened, Warren?" Sid asks, opening his eyes wide for the first time.

"Your nephew say you ain't gonna pay me."

"Why not?"

"He sat on his ass, that's why!"

Warren swipes the air with his fist. "I ain't telling you again—shut your fucking mouth!"

I kick the trash can across the room. "You don't tell me anything!"

He sucks in his breath, his whole face quivers, then he lunges across Sid and smashes me on the chin. His fist bores into my chest, pounding again and again. I'm knocked back against the desk while Willie and Esther struggle to hold him back.

"I want my money!"

"Okay," says Sid, "okay." He opens his wallet and takes out five dollars. "Here—all right?"

"Yeah."

"Go home now." Sid spreads one of his hands on the desk for support and massages his heart with the other, panting for breath. "Please, Warren, go home now."

"I'm working tomorrow, right?"

"Yes, yes, fine." He puts a cigar in Warren's pocket and pushes him toward the door.

"You and me, we worked together before this . . ." Warren climbs the stairs and then yells down from the top, "Just tell him not to be messin' with me or I'll kick his ass again!"

I sit on the floor, yanking at the lace of a shoe that has somehow been pulled off. My jaw is starting to swell. Above me stands Esther, a loose grip on my shirt. No one talks. Sid hands out the checks and everyone starts to leave in silence.

"Where you going?" he asks.

Willie slams his fist on the doorway and whirls around.

"We're gone, Sid! Work's done."

"What work? We're going out for a drink." He checks his wallet. "I'm buying."

No one moves.

"I'm serious, let's go." He claps his hands and looks down at me. "Everyone!"

"Holy shit, Sidney's gonna buy us a drink!"

"Where you taking us, Sid?" Esther asks.

"Marvin's"

"Man, that's a delicatessen."

"They got beer there, don't they?"

I sit motionless on the floor. More than my jaw, my chest hurts. I can't understand how I got here. I shouldn't be on the floor forcing back tears and rage, but somehow I'm down here.

"Quit moping, boy!" Willie snaps at me. "Get up! We're going drinking. It past time already!"

We walk down the street: Oliver carrying the *Daily News,* Willie with his arm around me telling me who the 76ers should sign this year, and Sid walking beside Esther asking her if he doesn't always treat her right. The sidewalk opens up ahead. Heat rises up like helium through my body, lessening the density, making me lose track of when this all began. The light changes. Willie jerks me toward him. Our shoulders bump as we cross.

Other Lives

The sun had dropped behind the mountains, and the We-Curl-Up-And-Dye-For-You Beauty Salon had closed its doors and Venetian blinds for the evening. Paul's skin tingled in the dry heat, so different from the suffocating humidity back East, yet the sun was almost too intense, stinging out here, always making him squint even with sunglasses.

He was getting married the day after tomorrow in Tucson and had driven all the way out from New Jersey, only to break down fifty miles south of Albuquerque in this small town. A hasty turn off the interstate, when his temperature gauge needle leaned toward hot, had led him through miles of empty desert before he found a gas station.

"This is what we're going to do," the mechanic said. "I'll call the dealer in Albuquerque and see if he can ship the part down on the next bus." The mechanic's name, Freddie Mendez, was stitched in blue on his white shirt. Little wedges were cut in the short sleeves to accommodate his biceps.

"What if it doesn't get here in time tonight?"

"Don't worry. I'll get you fixed up. I'll stay here until we get the job done."

The next bus from Albuquerque would be in at 7 P.M. Freddie, who had called the two auto parts stores in town but hadn't been able to find a water pump, would meet the bus and pick up the part C.O.D. Then he'd bring it back to the station, put the new pump in Paul's Toyota, and "You tie that knot right on schedule," Freddie said, winking at him.

The El Rey Motel was next door, across from the beauty salon, and Paul decided he'd go there to take a nap for a few hours until the car was ready. Then he'd drive through the night to Tucson and surprise Nora early in the morning. Having taken a plane, Nora was already in Tucson to help prepare for the wedding. The plan had been that Paul would bring the car out and they'd drive to San Francisco for their honeymoon, then continue up the coast into Canada and spend the rest of the summer sightseeing and camping, making a big loop back to New Jersey.

After he checked into the motel (a Pakistani with an incessant smile was the manager and gave him a room facing the street), Paul stretched out on the bed, intending to take only a short nap. Talking to Nora would make him feel better. Yesterday she had told him in breathless words about going to the florist, the caterer, the minister, the seamstress, punctuating each sentence with I miss you so much I could *scream* and then had done so, loudly, into the phone. Her controlled hysteria was familiar, surprisingly comforting. It hadn't really sunk in—that he was actually getting married—until Nora had left on the plane and he'd gone out shopping for a suit, Nora forbidding him to wear to the wedding his old corduroy coat with its worn, indistinguishable waling and his loafers, the uniform he'd taught Introduction to Logic in as a graduate assistant in philosophy for the last three years.

He'd bought a blue suit. The woman who helped him pick it out—she was at least sixty—had said You'll look just like my husband did the day we got married. He's dead now, a heart attack. But we were married for forty years, happy every one of them. Then he died before me. You'd think after all that time he could have waited. Don't *you* run out on your wife like that now, she joked—only Paul didn't think she was joking. It was the extent of what marriage meant; there was a whole new and involuntary way to desert someone, a fresh set of rules that had little to do with sharing an apartment as he and Nora had done the last two years. There they'd been alone when they were separated, together when together, and now they would be together when alone and apart only when they died, if then, he thought—and not very nicely so, if you were to believe the woman who had dressed him. (I'm sorry I can't be there to get you all spruced up she had said, actually pinching his cheek to get a little color into it because she was sure he'd have some ruddiness in his face, being the wedding was in Tucson, and she wanted to see how his rose coloring would go with the pearl-gray tie.)

He had come away from the experience of buying the suit not thinking of marriage as a nestled, secure place but more of a layaway plan, something the woman had suggested he could do with his suit before she found out they weren't having the usual long engagement of a year (which she pleasantly remembered of her own situation). He couldn't shake the feeling until he actually started the trip out—their marriage a slow, swinging, naked light bulb, their private set of parallel lines stretching to infinity, the quiet tick tock of his heart beating alongside Nora's into eternity. But then, driving through Ohio one night, he'd pulled the car off the road and fallen asleep in a farmer's field outside Zanesville. In the morning, cows were walking by, their udders swinging within tickling distance of his nose. He had put his sleeping bag down in the middle of their path. Jumping up, he ran from the massive creatures—on his back he had pictured a slow, crushing, bovine death—then stopped to laugh. They were completely harmless. The farmer, the owner of the cows, Paul guessed, waved a good morning from off in the distance on his tractor, his dog sitting alongside him. The cows' udders were heavy and full with milk, the fields were green with high corn, the sky was the burnished copper-blue of early summer mornings. Every living thing was in its place and he was going to be married soon, completely in love.

When he woke up it was already dark. Someone was knocking.

A woman stood at the door. "Freddie said I should tell you that the pump didn't come in on the 7:05 and he's going to see if it gets here on the 10:10. Oh," she said and pushed right by him to the air conditioner in the window. She stood in front of it and flapped her blouse up and down. "It's as hot as a pig's bladder out there."

He couldn't believe this. His car wasn't ready, it was dark, and now this woman was in his motel room.

She sat down on the edge of the bed, with her back to him and fanned her skirt in front of the air conditioner, the same way she'd done her blouse.

"When will my car be ready?"

"I told you. Ten o'clock the next bus comes in."

"Is that the last one?"

"Yup."

"Jesus," Paul mumbled to himself. If it wasn't on that one . . . he didn't want to think about it. Tomorrow was Saturday: he'd have to leave the car, catch a bus up to Albuquerque, fly to Tucson for his wedding and then somehow get back here. All their plans to drive straight to San Francisco and on to Canada would need to be changed. "Excuse me," he said. "I think I'll go see Freddie about my car."

"Why? Nothing's happened yet. It's still sitting in the same spot. He can't do nothing until the bus comes in."

Paul sat down on the other twin bed, the one with a picture of a sad harlequin above it. The bedspreads were a pink, nubby material. The woman, a strawberry blonde, turned the cross around her throat to the back of her neck. "I'm Ray," she said. "Freddie's sister-in-law. Frankie and I own the diner across the street. Frankie is Freddie's twin brother."

"Oh," Paul said.

"You want to hear about my wedding?"

"What?"

"You're going to be married, aren't you? That's what Freddie said."

Nora! He'd forgotten to call Nora! She'd be worried about him. "I need to make a phone call."

"Go right ahead."

"In private."

"Well, all right then." She flapped her blouse a couple more times as she went by the air conditioner. "Your friends going to play any tricks on you?"

"Tricks?"

"You know, wedding tricks. Like our friends did. That's what I wanted to tell you. We stayed in the Holiday Inn down the road on our honeymoon night and let me tell you, we had a real good time that night, real good."

Paul was standing with his hand on the door. Ray was walking around the room picking up things and setting them back down. "It really was kind of mean what they done. I thought one day I'd look back on it all and get a good laugh, but it hasn't been that way. Frankie developed some problems, to tell the truth. He has to lock all the doors and check around everywhere and well, by that time, I'm a little out of the mood, especially when he gets up to look right in the middle of things. I mean, I thought they was going to surprise us, but not by hiding under the bed."

"What!"

"Sure," Ray said. "There was the two of them, Mike and Luis. When we got up in the morning they crawled out from under our bed."

"My God," Paul said.

A strand of her hair had slipped down in her face, and she made a loud PHFFFFFT blowing it up from her eyes.

"So I always tell people—it's a kind of public service from me—to check under the bed on your matrimonial night. What's she like?"

"Who?"

"Your wife to be."

"I really have to make this phone call," Paul said.

"To her?"

"Yes, to her."

"To be honest, the magic's gone. We've been going on ten years now and I got to admit we lost something. Sure we had our share of the good moments but they just get harder to come by as you go along. I guess I don't have to tell you that. You look old enough to have learned a *couple* things by and by. How old are you anyway?"

"Twenty-seven," Paul said.

"You think it's going to be different for you. I know you do. I can tell by looking at your eyes that you think we're all dummies around here."

"I don't think that."

"It's all right if you do. And maybe I am a dummy. I could be doing a lot better than I am. You should've seen me draw. I won all the prizes. That's what I was going to do before I met Frankie, was be an art teacher. I thought I'd settle down in some little town with maple trees along the street, somewhere far away as you can get from this damn place, and I'd marry somebody intelligent. Like you maybe."

"Me!"

"Just like you. Somebody with a nice serious mouth who'd look at my pictures and say how smart I was to be able to draw like that."

"Well, I—"

"It's all right. I'm not trying to say anything here. Just so you know. I got to go now, too. I left some customers waiting at their tables to come over here and talk with you."

Paul moved aside. "I appreciate your telling me."

"No, you don't," Ray said, "but that's okay, too. *I* feel better."

Ray strode across the street, calling "I'm coming! Hold your water!" to a man who must have been Frankie, standing in a grease-smudged apron, a perpetual, dark stare, his eyes slitted, watching.

Paul picked up the phone, but somebody was on the line: "I *told* him, I want him to spray the whole place and get rid of all them little eggs . . ."

"Hello? Hello?" Paul said.

There was silence on the other end of the phone, then, "Who is this?"

"Excuse me, but I believe you're on my line," Paul said.

"Your line!"

"Who's that you're talking to, Leanore?" a male voice said.

"It's some guy who's cutting in our conversation."

"Are you at this motel?" Paul said.

"Hey, fella!" the male voice said. "Who's this guy, Leanore?"

"I don't know, honey, he just cut right in . . ."

Paul went to the front desk. The Pakistani was still there. "Excuse me," Paul said, "but I was trying to make a phone call from my room and someone's on the line."

The Pakistani looked at the switchboard. "Yes, that is right, sir," he said. "She be off soon and then you make your call."

"Why didn't you tell me you had only one line for the phones?"

"Because we have two," the Pakistani said and smiled brightly.

Paul went back to the room and sat with his head in his hands. He had to get out of this town—tonight. Carefully, quietly, he picked up the receiver again: "So I told him, get it straight, we ain't the little people you all are looking for . . ."

Little people? Eggs? He listened to the conversation a while longer but couldn't make any sense of it, no matter how hard he tried. Other people's lives were so strange. Were there little people staying somewhere in the motel—and what did this have to do with eggs?

He would use the pay phone at the station and see about his car at the same time. Outside, the air was still hot and he felt the dust settle in the back of his throat. The lights of Ray's diner went off across the street. He walked to the gas station but it was closed. No one was around. Freddie had deserted him! The Toyota, still in the same spot, sat with its hood open. Anybody could have come in here and stripped the parts!

Across the street, Paul saw the door open and Frankie step out. Frankie looked up, his eyes black and furious, then he stumbled forward a few feet and fell face down in the street, with a knife in his back.

Ray ran into the street crying "Baby baby baby baby" and collapsed on top of Frankie. Paul said, "Jesus Christ!" and hurried to the motel office to call for help, but no one was there. Meanwhile an ambulance pulled up, its siren screaming, and Frankie, still breathing, groaning—the knife had gone under his shoulder blade—was placed on a stretcher and taken away. The cops handcuffed Ray and pushed her wailing into the police car. Her face squished against the glass, she was trying to tell Paul something. "What?" Paul said. He bent closer, unable to hear in all the noise. Before he could make out anything, the police car started up and took her away with its lights flashing.

What did she say? Maybe it was Freddie, call Freddie? He looked around; Freddie was nowhere in sight. Or did she want him, Paul, to come to the police station? He walked across the street to the gas station, still locked up. His car was in the same place. It was nine-thirty. He had a little time before the bus came in—but what then? Where would Freddy be? And how would he ever get the car fixed in this mess? Ray had stabbed her husband; Freddy was nowhere to be found; there were little people in the motel, eggs and God knows what else; and he was stuck here for who knew how long. He'd call Nora.

When he got back to the motel room, he opened the door and found a couple inside. The man had his shirt unbuttoned and the woman stuck her head out from the bathroom when the door opened. "What the fuck . . ." the man said and crouched down, his right hand extended, ready to chop Paul up like cole slaw. Except the guy looked fat and out of shape, balding and a little crocked too. "Your ulcer, Mel!" the woman said.

"My room," Paul said. "This is my room—"

The woman screamed when the man thrust his leg out several times—he looked more as if he were trying to knock a small dog off his cuff than executing a karate kick—and Paul closed the door and went to see the Pakistani again.

The Pakistani was gone. A young woman, gorgeous Paul thought, with long straw-blonde hair and a bright orange halter across her chest, was thumbing through credit card receipts. "Somebody's in my room," Paul started, but didn't get far because the Pakistani came out from behind the curtains of the motel office. The smell of curry wafted after him and Paul caught a glimpse of a living room and a tiny kitchen. Still chewing, the Pakistani dabbed at his mouth with a linen napkin. He put his hand around the blonde's waist—was she his wife, at least thirty years younger than he?—and moved her aside. "I thought you check out, sir. You say you check out this evening. I look in room and find no baggage there."

"But I haven't gone yet, and my bags are in the car which is at the gas station. Freddie's supposed to be repairing it. Didn't you hear the commotion outside? Ray stabbed her husband, Frankie." He felt as if he were explaining a preposterous soap opera to foreigners. "Didn't you hear what was going on?"

"I do not hear, sir," the Pakistani said.

"But surely you must know Ray? She's right across the street— and Freddie? They're your neighbors!"

The Pakistani shook his head. "We do not know people here. We come from Oregon to manage motel. You wish to have dinner with us?"

The blonde blinked at Paul; it was a completely sexless look.

"Sorry," Paul said. "I can't." He looked at the star-shaped, gold-plated clock above the doorway that led to the back of the motel's office, where the Pakistani lived with the stunning blonde. For some reason he imagined them sleeping chastely on a tatami mat, the blonde kissing the Pakistani sweetly on the forehead before they meditated and fell asleep. "Could you direct me to the bus station?"

The Pakistani said no; the blonde just shrugged her thin shoulders that stayed up around her neck a few moments before she let them drop with a melodious sigh and went back to the credit card receipts.

At 10:10 exactly the bus from Albuquerque pulled in. Freddie was nowhere to be found, but Paul hadn't expected him here. He was probably at the hospital with his brother, and for a moment, as Paul watched the bus unload, he thought, *I should be there too.*

He went and asked the bus driver if an auto part had been sent down on the trip. The driver checked the baggage compartment and pulled out a tightly sealed box addressed to Freddie's service station. "That's for me," Paul said. "It's for my car."

The driver eyed him suspiciously but was willing to relinquish the package when Paul agreed to pay the C.O.D. charges. Finally, he could leave. In the morning he'd find another mechanic and have the part put in—or do it himself. He could see how the old one was connected and follow the steps.

But as he turned the corner to return to the motel, he saw Freddie's truck with its giant mud tires. Maybe he could get Freddie to take just a few minutes and install the pump. Waving his arms, Paul stepped into the street. A second too late it occurred to him that Freddie had just learned the bad news and must be speeding to the hospital. Paul saw his life flash before his eyes, except it was the other life, the double one that is always beside us, then he stepped out of the way of Freddie's truck just in time. The truck screeched to a halt halfway down the street. Freddie threw the vehicle into reverse and wheeled back for Paul. Except when the truck pulled alongside Paul it wasn't Freddie driving at all, but a midget—sitting on several telephone books. "You Paul?" the midget said.

"Yes."

"Freddie said I should come get you and fix your pump. He said you might be here. That the part?"

"Yes," Paul said, ecstatic. He'd soon be on his way to Tucson and could marry Nora, normal Nora, so normal compared to these people he didn't know how he would ever explain any of this to her.

Paul hopped in the truck and the midget, who was using a metal rod to push the gas pedal, sped off down the street. A wooden box sat between them on the seat, and with its metal latch and holes in the top, there could have been a bird or small animal inside. "What's in here?" Paul said.

The midget looked down at the box.

"Don't tell me," Paul said. "Eggs, right? Eggs?" He started to laugh. "Are you related to Freddie?" Paul asked, seeing that the midget was not amused.

"I'm not related to nobody," the midget said. There was no conversation after that. The midget seemed loath to talk. They reached the gas station and Paul saw that the lights of the station were still off but his car was gone. "My car!"

"Where'd you leave it?"

"Right here! Right here!" He pointed to a spot in the parking lot that had no more than an oil stain on it now. "Somebody stole my car!"

"You'd better call the authorities," the midget said. "I can't work on your car until it's here."

Paul walked around in a circle where the car had been. The midget, who had a craggy face and sideburns that came to sharp razor points in front, said that Freddie was always doing this to him.

"What? Doing what? Stealing cars!"

"I'm not going to talk with you if you yell at me. My pastor doesn't allow people to yell at me."

"Your pastor, what does he have to do with this?"

"You'd better call the authorities," the midget said.

He seemed petulant about the fact that Paul hadn't called the authorities.

"Jesus," Paul said and went next door to the Pakistani's motel again. The blonde was still at the desk and when Paul rang the night bell she came to the door and let him in. "My car's been stolen," Paul said. "Stolen!"

"No," the blonde said.

"What do you mean, no? Did you see someone take it?"

"Yes. That man you told us about, Freddie. From next door. He came over here and asked if we had seen you."

"*Freddie* has my car?" Paul leaned toward the blonde to hear her answer. She had a kind of compelling gravity, that neutered pleasantness that comes of interest in one's soul but nothing else. It made him want to flirt with her, drop innuendoes, leer with greasy insincerity . . . what in the world was wrong with him! He was getting married in another day! He withdrew from the counter.

"We told him you went to the bus station."

"Oh, God," Paul said and slumped down in one of the chairs. "I can't go on like this. Please, I beg you. I must use your phone." She led him into the back, the small room with the train kitchen, a legless sofa next to the phone. Nora's phone rang unanswered, three, four, five . . . ten times. Paul put his head back against the wall and began to moan softly.

The blonde came back through the beaded curtain. She was wearing a long calico skirt that drooped to her bare feet. She knelt down and started to unlace his shoes.

"What are you doing?"

"Your headache. I'll rub your feet and take away your headache."

A headache, yes, now that she mentioned it he did have a headache. He let her massage his foot with her strong hands, her warm fingers, more than let her, murmured and sighed, groaned and would have wept it felt so good to be caressed, even on his feet. He put his head back. He had to leave by twelve tonight. That would give him barely enough time. He kept trying to open his eyes but the soothing touch of her fingers—now she was just stroking the top of his foot—kept making him drift off. He saw Nora. She was waiting for him in Tucson; he could see her very clearly in the church; they had started without him. "He'll be here," Nora's father, Mr. Bildings, said. "Paul's a responsible young man. Have no worry, dear." And what about his own parents? Yes, they were there, too, in the front row, his mother not nearly as decked out in jewels as Nora's mother, not nearly as sophisticated or rich or . . . happy. Yes, so unhappy, crippled with arthritis, spending their precious savings on this trip . . . all for him.

"Marry me," he said, but as if in a stupor. He felt drugged, only the delicious pressure of the blonde's—what was her name, why hadn't he asked her name, so rude of him—thumb on the bottom of his sole, how gentle and probing at the same time, how deep and ticklish, he had to know who she was, who was she . . . ?

He marries the blonde, of course, and the Pakistani gives her away. The minister says, "Do you, Paul, take this blonde to be your lawfully wedded wife?" I do. "Do you, blonde, take Paul to be your lawfully wedded husband?" The blonde smiles. She does not speak. Her consent is communicated telepathically. It is a marriage made in . . . this town whose name Paul cannot remember, or pronounce even if he could remember. The midget's pastor bows his head. The blonde raises her face to receive her wedding kiss, cool, beckoning, white, blemishless, silent. Till death do us part.

"Amigo! I've been looking everywhere for you!"

Paul opened his eyes. Freddie was standing in front of him. The blonde was gone.

"It wasn't your water pump after all, just a bad gasket in the thermostat."

The car was waiting outside, its engine idling. Freddie had filled the gas tank. Paul's bags were still in the back where he'd left them.

"Go!" Freddie said. "Hurry, man!"

He wanted to know about Frankie, about Ray . . . were they all right? And where was the blonde? He needed to say goodbye to her, thank her for the massage, tell her . . . something about how he felt, or apologize maybe. Had he acted improperly? It didn't seem real to him, that he would leave now, that he hadn't always been among these people. What did their lives have to do with his? What did anyone's life really have to with another person's?

Three years later, on their way up to Crater Lake for a vacation, Nora would turn to him one day and say, "What really happened in that town?" Paul was already an assistant professor of philosophy at the University of California, Santa Cruz, where the Toyota had died (finally) en route to their honeymoon in San Francisco. Stuck in Santa Cruz unexpectedly for two days, they had fallen in love with the town, and looked back on the Toyota's demise as fortunate.

"I broke down."

"The car?"

"No, me. There was a kind of breakdown—not entirely unpleasant."

Nora suddenly seized Paul's arm; he had to grab the wheel tightly to keep from swerving. "I just felt the baby kick. I'm sure of it, Paul."

They pulled off the side of the road near a picnic table. "Can I feel?" and Nora took his hand and placed it on her stomach. He imagined he felt a fluttering movement too, a sensation—not unlike the feathery touch of the blonde's lips—that he associated with the invisible, the unknown, and the forgotten.

Legacy

David had taken to riding the buses at night, which would bring him all the way to the edge of Philadelphia if he stayed on long enough. His father wasn't home much anymore and his sister had gone to Michigan for the summer to live with their cousin, a girl of twelve like herself. It was on one of these bus rides, these round trips late at night, the last run before the driver took the bus back to the barn, that David flattened himself against the huge front window and projected himself into the depths of space. The driver had turned off his lights on an isolated, moonless, empty stretch of road, letting David fall into such a deep tar of black space that he burst into tears. He had not felt anything since his mother was hospitalized and he was grateful to this black bus driver. A bond, an instinctive trust, had sprung up between the two of them from the first. No questions were asked. What was he doing out so late? Why was a sixteen-year-old boy riding around on buses all the time? Instead, the driver let him ride every night for free, in fact, seemed to enjoy the company and shared his "night lunch," insisting that David keep up his strength for the long evening. "It gonna be a slow night."

At one A.M., David would hop off the bus shortly before it pulled into the barn, the pneumatic doors hissing.

He came in late one night and heard his father arguing on the phone: *I can't see you now, don't call here again like this . . .*

His father, after he hung up, was surprised then upset to discover David downstairs. "And where have you been?"

"Riding buses."

"I want you inside this house by eleven unless it's a special occasion."

"Define special occasion."

"A date. A school event. A party or a prom. An activity that normal young people are doing. What is this thing with riding buses?"

"I like them," David said matter-of-factly. He delighted in the hugeness, the loud whining and gnashing of gears, the hearty expulsion of exhaust from the bowels, the slow, ponderous, dinosaur starts and stops: an anachronistic beast in an age of cyclotrons and lasers, a crude, gross, lumbering mass of molecular junk.

"By eleven," his father said. "Remember."

But not long after this conversation his father began staying out late, too—or not coming home at all. The answering machine became the principal form of communication between them. "Hello, Dad, I won't be home for dinner, so don't expect me." And his father would call in with his own message. "I'm working late this evening so don't wait up for me, David. Don't forget to call your mother." Which he did, dutifully, every night, although his mother would hardly talk. Two weeks had passed since he'd seen her; the doctor said she needed the time apart from the family to orient herself.

David would mechanically run down what he'd done in school and how her collection of orchids was doing (he was now taking care of them) and what he'd decided to do about the pigeons on the roof (a rubber snake, the bus driver told him—"It scare them flying rats right off!") and at the end of the conversation he would tell her, "I have to go now, Mom, I love you," and she would answer in the same flat featureless voice that he remembered her speaking in the day she had her breakdown, "Goodbye, David," and her face to him would become smooth and blank as white wax.

His sister and he had found her staring out the window in her room, still in her bathrobe at 3 P.M. She'd been there all day. She didn't turn around when they crept in. "Are you all right, Mom?" his sister asked but their mother's face was so pale that David called his father. She didn't recognize David's father, thought he was her father, David's grandfather, dead for years now. A doctor at the hospital referred her to a psychiatrist who told them she was suffering severe depression, almost catatonia. "She's in pieces," he said. "She needs time, a safe place, and care to put herself back together." He recommended a residential treatment center on thirty peaceful acres.

"Thank you for calling, Abe." She had worked her way up to this. The polite voice could have been anyone. She sounded more like the receptionist at the doctor's office (who had just given him an appointment for a checkup—he was having painful indigestion). We'll see you next Thursday, then, Mr. Lorber. Same tone, same distance. His own wife. Thank you for calling, Abe.

She hadn't recognized him when he'd rushed home from work. Maury, she called him. Her father. She worshipped her father. Maury this, Maury that. Maury cooked wonderful meals, Maury told the funniest jokes. There was this tailor, this shoemaker, and this bellhop . . . Who could remember how it went? The tailor pricks his finger one day. The shoemaker mashes his thumb . . . Hopeless. He couldn't tell a joke if his life depended on it. Make me laugh, she'd say. Come on, Abe, tell me something funny. What was funny at two A.M.? Tell me a story, Abe. She'd curl up against him. He couldn't even keep his eyes open. A story? It's two A.M. Tell me a funny story. What kind of story is funny at two A.M.? Tell me about your aunt. What about her? You know, her invention. Oh, that. Embarrassing. He'd been raised by his mother, sister, and maiden aunt, three women. His mother wore fat wigs spilling with curls, like Marie Antoinette from Flatbush. His aunt thought she was an inventor. A rolling pin that played "Twinkle Twinkle Little Star." Elbow resters—little rubber cups to put your elbows in when you sat at the table, matching sets of eight. And his sister . . . she thought she ran the house, too. Do this, do that. Don't bring mud in here. Take a chicken over to your Aunt Bebe for dinner. (His aunt owned a secondhand furniture store and worked on her inventions in back.)

Meanwhile, his father had gone off to Jersey with another woman. He didn't even know his father had left for good until he'd gone to school one day, eight years old, and a little girl there said, "Your daddy is going to hell." An Irish girl—what did she know about his daddy? He hit her. For two days he had to hide in the rabbi's cellar. The Irish kids were going to beat him up. They threw rocks at his mother's house. The little girl's parents came to his door with a policeman. Terrible. Such terrible times. His mother crying. His aunt yelling at him in Yiddish. His sister, fourteen, frightened to go outside their row house in Philadelphia. No men around anywhere. Except him. And what was he doing? Hiding in the rabbi's cellar. Terrible times. Just as well never to think of such things now.

Did she wear them all the time?

What?

The shoes. Did she wear them around the house?

Aunt Bebe. Ruth was fascinated by her. Aunt Bebe had invented shoes that would wax the floor when you tap danced. His mother would play the piano while Bebe followed right along in her shoes. Both women worked themselves into a frenzy, Bebe making sparks on the floor she was jumping so much, and his mother banging away at the piano. At the end Bebe would collapse, her feet over the arm of the couch, the collection of springs and buffing pads on the soles of her shoes bent and ruined. The floor looked a mess, blotches of wax everywhere, a disaster area, worse than any mine field. "Just needs a little perfecting," she'd say. He'd look at his aunt panting and his mother still playing a finale. Such crazy women.

A few people sat outside in the late spring sunshine, warming themselves on the patio. Behind them was a picture window with its awning unfurled. The grounds, smelling of freshly cut grass, rolled off into the distance, where a split-rail fence marked the boundaries of the treatment center. It looked like a resort

David had gone to with his parents and sister, Tina, in the Poconos—complete with a pool, unused at the moment.

"I'll tell you something, this is the best," his father said. Which meant that he'd paid a lot of money to put her here. Which meant he felt guilty about paying so much money but not as guilty as he did about putting her here in the first place. Which meant he wanted David to say something that was roughly the equivalent of a thank you, since his mother certainly wasn't going to and needed a stand-in.

"It looks comfortable."

"You bet it is. Believe me, with what you pay here in one week you could take a vacation around the world. I'm not complaining. Just so you should know what we're doing for your mother."

"Thank you," David said. His father nodded.

They went inside to the reception area and a woman at the counter asked if she could help.

"Ruth Lorber. Her husband and—" his father thrust David forward— "boy to see her. She's expecting us. This is quite a facility you've assembled."

"I'll page your wife, Mr. Lorber," the receptionist said. David winced at his father's nervousness: the need to take control, even here, and pretend he knew his way around.

They took seats in the waiting area. Not stiff plastic chairs in chewy vitamin colors but soft earth-tone couches with brushed upholstery. A girl about his age, in white shorts and a black leotard top, walked into the lobby, suddenly stopped and turned around to the empty hallway. "Oh, fuck you, just fuck you, too!"

"Regina," the receptionist said. "That's five. You're on Q-call after this."

"Who gives a dick head," Regina said and kicked open the outside door. Her laugh, which sounded like an exotic multi-colored parrot, carried back over her shoulder.

"Whew," David's father said. "Some mouth. I hope your mother isn't exposed to that kind of thing too much."

*   *   *

The doctor wanted to meet with him privately. In the meantime, David could wait in the canteen.

Inside the doctor's office they sat together on a couch. Did he want some coffee? Tea? No, nothing.

"Mr. Lorber—"

"Abe."

"Abe, Ruth is making progress. She's not starving herself as she did when she first arrived. She eats regularly now and even participates in some of the activities. She especially likes working with ceramics in OT and is quite talented according to her instructor."

"What's OT?"

"Occupational therapy. Sorry. I don't mean to throw terms at you."

The doctor wore a baggy sweater and blue jeans and looked fifteen years younger than himself, yet Abe knew they were roughly the same age. You could bet the man didn't wake up in the middle of the night holding his kishkas from belching so hard. An ulcer. He knew that's what it was. Heaven help him it shouldn't be bleeding.

"Her problem right now is that she's angry and frightened of what will happen if that anger is turned loose. Especially on her children. These are real fears for her, that she's going to harm someone. She has a lot of resentment stored up."

"Against me?"

"I want you to know that I'm not judging you, but yes, that is much of what she's dealing with now."

Coming through the French doors that led from the patio, she had embraced David first, then said, How are you, Abe? and touched his cheek lightly with hers. How nervous he was! He hadn't realized it—how much he expected her to act strange or drugged or be a zombie and scare him to death with a wordless stare.

Prim she looked. She sat on the edge of the chair. Her hands made into little fists on her knees. She'd gained some weight, which was good. Her hair was up, off her neck. She'd worn it down for years. Only when they were engaged did he ever remember it up like that. It was fastened in back with a red barrette he'd never seen. He fixed on it because it was the one thing about her that showed another life, the piece that represented the missing two weeks—something she had done that he didn't know about. For all the reality of her being here, he had imagined he knew her life so well that he could fill in this frightening gap. He'd coped with her absence through a belief that she was in a parallel yet known world and nothing had changed. Except he'd left out this barrette. And all that was behind it.

"I know I haven't been the best husband but I'm willing to change, doctor. You tell me what to do and I'll do it. I'll do anything to make her better again."

"Our view here is that each family member is part of a system. We need to work with the whole system to help the individual. So I'd like you to be part of Ruth's therapy. And for David and Tina to participate."

"How much time would that involve?"

"Would that matter?"

He turned away from the doctor to belch, excused himself. "My stomach, I'm having some problems from this."

"Yes, I would expect so. It must be a terrific strain on you."

"Not so bad."

"Bad enough I bet."

He felt his eyes moisten. "I haven't told anybody about this. Her family, nobody. I can't tell them she's here."

"Why not?"

"I don't know. I can't tell them, that's all. They'd worry. They'd want to know why."

"Why can't you tell anyone?"

He looked away. "In my opinion—and this is only my opinion, doctor—what my wife needs most is a good rest and someone to listen to her thoughts, help her make sense of them."

"We were talking about you, Abe."

He remembered how his Aunt Bebe and mother and sister all used to surround him when he'd done something bad. Hitting the little Irish girl. Why'd you do it! What kind of thing is that

for a boy like you to do! You should be ashamed of yourself!
You have to be a little man around here now!

"You want to know something, doctor? All right, I'll tell you
something!"

He started to sob.

Her hands had shaken when she reached over to button down
David's collar. He'd purposely left it undone. Kids at school
were wearing them like that now. Still, he was delighted with
her fussing, a hope that maybe she was herself and would come
home soon. Her shaky fingers fiddled with the collar and she
asked about Wayne, the dog, and whether they were eating good
meals at night. (Soup and cheese sandwiches, that's all he
wanted, and his father's stomach couldn't take anything else.)
She had letters on her lap from David's sister. Anybody else
would have thought she was the most content wife and mother
in the world.

His father wanted to know about the food, her room, the
activities, did she have enough to read, look what they had
brought—a corned beef on rye from Leon's. You can bet you
won't find that here! Oh, and David's got something, too. He
presented his mother with a gold watch they had picked out.
Just to keep your spirits up, from all of us. There was a small
card inside that said, WE MISS YOU!, complete with a paw
print from Wayne. His mother held the corned beef sandwich
in one hand and the watch in the other and looked back and
forth between them and began crying. His father stood up nervously. He patted her shoulder. "Why don't you show us around,
Ruth?"

Afterward she went to her room to rest.

The girl in the white shorts and black leotard walked into
the canteen.

David quickly knelt down and began tying his shoe. Her
footsteps came closer and he kept his head bent, pulling slowly
at the laces, hoping she would leave.

"That's a silly way to ignore somebody." She was standing
above him.

"What?" David said. Her chest stuck out like a roof—almost to the coke machine behind him. That's how close she was.

"Are you scared of me?"

"No," David said. He stood up. She was a little taller than he. "Should I be?"

"You're acting scared. Your shoulders are hunched, your knees are bent, you're not making eye contact, and your shoe's still untied."

He could smell her, her hair and skin, what a strong scent—not perfume like his mother—just her body and its heat, puffing at him like a bellows, the black leotard tight across her chest.

She reached in the back pocket of the baggy white shorts and took out a rumpled pack of cigarettes, lit one. "My last," she said, "before naughty Regina loses her smoke privileges."

"For what you said in the hallway?"

"You heard that, huh? Nah. For some other things. More naughty things." She blew the smoke along the side of his face. He felt it whiz by his ears. "I'm just plain out of control. A status offender all the way, smoking, drinking, fucking . . . everything except voting under age."

"How old are you?"

She laughed. "Dumb question. Try another."

It was a dumb question. Who cared how old she was, how old anyone was around here.

"Do you know my mother?"

"Who is she?"

"Ruth Lorber."

"Ohhhh, Ruthie. Yeah, she and I are buddies. She tears up in OT. The woman should be a potter or something. You see her stuff?"

"No." He remembered how his mother had quickly taken them past the door marked Occupational Therapy. And in her room she had asked David not to open her closet, when, out of curiosity, he'd started to look inside.

"Yeah, she won't be here long. Not as long as me, anyway. I'm a regular Mother Superior around here with all my time.

So how about you? You a snarf, prep, hood, grease, punk, popper, rapper, dude, or veg?"

"I ride buses," David said.

Regina looked stumped.

"My father is talking to the doctor."

"Herr Doktor. Frankie."

"He seems nice."

"Frankie's a peach. A real Georgia peach. Come on, your father won't be done for a while."

Her room was a mess. Clothes scattered everywhere. Magazines all over the bed, which was on the floor. A couple of wet towels hung over the curtain rods. There were sheets of butcher paper on the wall with huge Chinese letters in thick purple paint. And lunch baggies taped wherever he looked. "What are those for?" David asked.

"Hey, *what are those for?*" she said, mimicking him.

"Did I ask the wrong question?"

"Can't you tell art, bus?"

He looked closer. The bags were filled with tiny plastic babies. "What is it? A statement about abortion?"

"God. Are you for real?" She was in the bathroom doing something—without the door closed. He was careful not to look.

"Nuclear war?"

She came out of the bathroom, in a beach shirt that barely covered her thighs. "Sorry, I don't mix politics and art." She shut the outside door.

She sat down on the end of the bed and pulled the shirt over her knees so it formed a big tent. He felt awkward standing around, but he couldn't look at the bags any longer, so he leaned against the wall with one foot flat against it, trying to act nonchalant.

"Scared?"

"No." But his heart was butting the inside of his chest. "Listen, I just came here to visit my mother. I don't even know you. My mother's two doors away taking a nap and my father's talking with the doctor who's head of this place. I don't feel very comfortable here."

"You're a cutie, you know that? I love your eyes."

She stretched out one tan leg. Her toes, the nails painted blue, pointed at him, and he could see down the long curve of her leg to white panties under her T-shirt. She stood up. In her bare feet she was the same height as he. She was so close that he smelled the smoke from her breath and saw how pink and moist her gums were, the lines—or maybe cuts—on her bottom lip, so close that a muscle in his neck jumped.

She pinned his wrists against the wall with the heels of her hands and pressed into him. A plastic baggy fell on his head. He felt his buttocks tighten like a fist and then their mouths were a slice of skin apart before he said, *I don't want to take advantage of you. I mean your being in here and all.* Or thought he said or heard someone say, and with a howling laugh she threw her head back and then plunged her tongue deep into his mouth.

He'd tried with David. God knows, he'd tried to get him interested in things, soccer, hockey, a little fixing up around the house, something they could do together. He couldn't help but be disappointed, he told the doctor. His own father had left when he was eight. All his life he'd looked forward to doing the things with a son that he'd never been able to do with his father. Sure, he knew it was wrong. It was one of the things he and Ruth argued about. Let the boy have his own life, she'd say. Take an interest in what he wants to do. So he tried. He'd ask David about his telescope, what he was doing. Searching, he'd say. For what? Strings. Strings? Cosmic strings. They're what tie the universe together. Good, he'd tell him. Keep looking. What kind of a conversation could you have with someone who thought there were strings that tied the universe together? Meanwhile, his daughter was killing herself trying to make an impression, dress up nice, get good grades, practice her ballet in every room where he happened to be reading the paper, and all he could notice was how his son walked with his feet out like a duck. Put your feet together, he'd yell at David. The boy would flush from the neck up and make his feet straight but five minutes later he'd be walking with his feet out again and his mind up in the clouds somewhere and his sister would still be jumping through the air with a smile nailed to her face.

He thought maybe with his daughter away for the summer and Ruth in the hospital, they'd be closer. But they were further apart than ever. The boy rode buses all night. And himself . . . he was not the best example of responsibility.

But that was over now, or it was going to be over.

She was a secretary in the office, going through a divorce. In one regard, he might as well have been going through a divorce himself, for months now. Who was he kidding? Years. Ruth didn't want him to touch her anymore and to tell the truth he wasn't attracted to her, although he couldn't remember which came first, her rolling away at nights or his falling asleep before she even finished in the bathroom. He thought maybe it might even help, put a little excitement back in his life, make him want Ruth more. At least that's what he told himself. And the worst thing was that it did.

They drove home in silence. His father clenched the wheel, silent, upset at something that neither he nor David wanted to discuss, that had to do with his mother and his sister and the doctor and all of them in therapy as sick people.

He was sick all right.

She'd thrust her shoulder into his teeth and drawn blood— from herself, a thin line of dark red blood. She smeared it on the tip of his penis and then rubbed him against her in all his limpness, his stickiness and shame at not even having his underpants off before he had ejaculated. He felt himself becoming hard again, then pushing inside, the utter exhilaration of his growing huge and her contracting at the same moment, a kind of dazzling love grip of the flesh: his skin was covered with wondrous eyes.

He came again in seconds and once more felt the hotness rush from below to his face and couldn't look at her until she told him he'd better go now and she had nothing on her face, absolutely nothing.

While he dressed, she washed herself in the bathroom, but this time with the door closed, which felt like a punishment. He was afraid he would cry for wanting to apologize and for just wanting to try again.

"I was nervous," he said when she came out, back in her white baggy shorts now and sitting on the opposite side of the room. "It's my first time."

"Oh, really?"

He cringed.

"You missed a loop," she said. He looked down and saw that he'd done so. "It goes on the inside, sweetie."

He started to redo his belt.

"Listen, you better go before I get caught. I'm in enough trouble as it is."

But he couldn't move; he wanted to say something that would explain. He stared hard at her, trying to deepen the contact. She had liked his eyes. "I'll be coming to see my mother. Maybe we could take a ride together in the country around here."

"On the bus, bus?"

"No, I'm getting my license in two weeks. I've already got a learner's permit."

"Sure thing." She turned away and lay on her side facing the wall, miserable or angry or, worse, indifferent. He didn't know. He put his hand on the metal door handle. Without a lock, it reminded him where he was.

"Well, I guess I'll see you." He was rooted to the spot; his face got redder watching her back rise and fall on the bed. She pulled a cover over her shoulder. He had touched her breasts, the pimpled skin around her woman's long nipples, been touching her ten minutes ago. He'd traveled so far inside her. She looked holy to him. "Thanks," he said.

Stupid, stupid, stupid, stupid. Thanks. How could he be so stupid. Thanks. Why not just throw money at her? Stupid stupid stupid *schmuck*.

*   *   *

His father wrapped his arms around him from behind and held him tight. They'd stopped at a driving range on the way home. "Let's hit some balls," his father had said. "You want to do that?" It was hardly a question. David nodded. He'd never played golf before. Never touched his father's clubs.

"Keep your eye on the ball. That's the important thing. Now take a swing." His father stepped back from him. It was the first time in years that he had hugged David, for any reason.

He swung hard but topped the ball and it rolled out to the grass.

"What did I tell you?" his father said. "What did I tell you about keeping your eye on the ball? Try again."

He did and connected better this time, although not with any flight.

"You're too stiff," his father said. He got behind him and formed his body over David's again, slapped his knee. "Bend that." David felt Regina slam his hands against the wall. "You can't get any lift on the ball unless you bend your leg there. And keep your left arm straight. Go slow. You're too jerky and fast. Slow."

He raised the club up slowly behind him, concentrating on the ball, and brought the iron down, his wrists tight. He hit the ball solidly. He watched it ascend in a handsome arc and drop down past the 150 mark.

"Terrific!" his father shouted. "Wonderful! Did you see the way you hit that? That's a professional shot!"

The praise was more than he could bear. He started to cry.

"What's wrong? You did good—what are you crying about?"

He turned away from his father, wiped his eyes with his sleeve. He was horribly embarrassed. "I'm going to the car," David said.

"Come here," his father said and grabbed him by the arm. "Just stay here with me while I hit some balls."

David stood to the side.

"You got a whole bucket of balls there you can take out your frustrations on," his father said. "That's why we came here." His father put a ball on the tee, raised the driver high behind him and smashed the ball in a line drive to the 225 mark. He put another one up and hit it even harder, grunting. A tractor, the driver protected in a wire cage, chugged along the grass retrieving balls. David's father seemed to be aiming for him. When he finished the basket, he was covered with sweat, his face flushed. He looked at David's full bucket. "Well, if you're not going to use them . . . we paid for them, after all."

And he emptied this bucket, too.

"I can't do anything right for you, can I? I bring you out here, show you how to do something physical and healthy, you do damn good your second try, and what happens? You stand there and sulk. What the hell is wrong with you?"

"I . . . "

"What?"

"I met someone. I met a girl while you were talking with the doctor."

His father laughed. "Good. She's a nice girl?"

Suddenly he could see how futile it was, to not be like his father. He was the same flesh and blood, the same genes, the same lies. The same fate. He'd done to someone what his father had done to his mother and what one day his son would do to someone all over again and there was no stopping it.

When his father went to the restroom, he ran toward the highway and stuck out his thumb, pleading for someone to stop. He would go back, apologize, end what was just beginning for him. He walked fast on the shoulder of the road and jerked his thumb in the air. A stone from a truck flew up and hit him, and he collapsed to the ground. Warm blood was on his hands. He couldn't see out of his right eye.

A car pulled up beside him. Someone said, "You hurt, son?" and then he heard his father's voice, "Here, he's my boy," and his father carried him to the car and put him in the front seat. His father said he was taking him to a hospital nearby, just hang on, we'll be there in five minutes. David covered his eye. He would wear a patch if he lost the eye. His father said something in Yiddish, but more as though he were talking to himself, and he realized his father was so scared he was praying.

Madagascar

This is a story I know so well.

My father, who is twenty-one, is on his way home from finding food for his family. He has traded a gold brooch for a bottle of milk, some vegetables and a little meat. With his blue eyes and blond hair, my father is the only one in the family who has any chance to pass for Gentile on the streets. He makes sure to sit on a public bench, to pick out a paper from the trash and look comfortable, then go on. Among the many edicts against Jews—no traveling in motor cars, no leaning out windows, no using balconies open to the street, no going outside after dark—is one that forbids them to sit on park benches.

On the way home he takes another chance meeting his fiancée in South Amsterdam. Before the deportations started they were to be married; now they must wait until the war ends, each of them hidden in different areas of the city.

After dark when he returns to the apartment cellar where his father, mother, and sister hide, he sees the Gestapo drive up. It is May 26, 1943. Tomorrow he will learn the Great Raid has taken away all the remaining Jews, those in rest homes, in mental institutions, in orphanages, those too sick to walk, those who have cooperated with the Germans thinking it would spare them. Even the entire Jewish Council will be shipped to the labor camps. Now he knows nothing, only that he must avoid the house, that if he is caught out after curfew he will be imprisoned or shot. He steps into a bakery where the baker—a Gentile though trusted friend of the family—offers to hide my father.

If someone has informed on the family and the Gestapo do not find all the members, the baker knows they will search the whole block; they have been through here before. They will check the back room, the bins of flour, the attic above. They will tap the floor and walls for any hollow spaces. But, ironically, they will not check the ovens.

The baker tells my father to climb into an oven no longer in use. At first my father resists. He is afraid. Afraid he will die in there. But there is no other way. The Gestapo will not think to look in such an obvious yet unlikely place.

My father crawls in. The sirens stop. His family is taken away to Majdanek, never to return. He lives in the oven until the end of the war, coming out every two hours when business has slowed sufficiently so that he may stretch. Some days the baker stays so busy that my father must be inside for three, four, and once even six hours. Without room to turn over or extend his legs, he remains curled up in a ball. On one occasion, much to his humiliation, he must go to the bathroom in his pants. The baker and his wife kindly provide him with a long apron while his trousers are washed in back. In the oven, he makes up waltzes in his head and has long, complex discussions with himself, marshaling arguments for each side, as to which of the two Strausses, father or son, is the true Waltz King, despite the son being known by the title. He re-creates each note of their compositions and discusses the works with a panel of experts, but always delays the final vote another day so he may weigh the evidence more carefully and reconsider the merits of "Joy and Greetings," "Lorelei-Rheinklange," "Shooting Stars," and a hundred others.

After the war my father will listen to music in a high-backed chair. The record player during my childhood, a hi-fi, will be near a whisper in volume, perhaps the loudness at which he originally heard the melodies in his head. When I come into the room, he does not mind being disturbed, but asks me to sit and listen with him. I am ten. "Ah, now," he says raising his hand when the French horns begin to play. "Our favorite part." I do not know if "our" includes me or someone else or if he just speaks of himself in the plural. Soon he closes his eyes, smiles and extends his hand for mine. Although we are sitting down, me at his feet, our arms sway together, my father waltzing with me from this position. Softly he releases my hand, tells me I have good timing and to remember practice practice practice. Mastering the clarinet is no easy task—even for a bright ten year old. He rises from his chair, pulls down the sides of his coat—on Sunday afternoons he wears a jacket and tie at home—returns the record to its sleeve, closes the lid of the hi-fi, and stands with his hands behind his back for a few seconds as though making a silent prayer. Then he says, "Ephram, would you like to accompany me on a walk in the park?" I have my coat on within five seconds.

In ninth grade, I am caught shoplifting. I steal a silver pen from a drugstore. I am taken to the police station in Haverford, the small town where we live outside Philadelphia and where my father teaches European history at Haverford College. My mother is in New York visiting her sisters, so I must call my father. The department secretary informs me that he should return from class within the hour.

"Are you at home, Ephram?"

"I'm at the police station," I say, shocked by my own admission. Perhaps I want to confess right away and get it over with, not hide the shame I feel, or perhaps I want to boast.

Without comment, she makes a note of my situation and promises she will get the message to my father immediately.

While I wait for my father in front of the sergeant's desk, on a plastic chair a faded aqua color, I think how I've wanted to succeed at something, most recently sports. The basketball game I made sure my father attended, positive I would be put in since we were playing a much weaker team, we wound up only narrowly winning, coming from behind. I sat on the bench the whole time. "Very stirring match," my father said afterward, walking me to the car, his arm around me. He knew I felt bad, of course, but there was nothing he could do, nothing I could do.

I lack the speed and agility to be first string; and by this season I have lost interest in sports, don't even try out for the team, and instead have fallen in with a group of kids who hang out at the edge of the parking lot, wear pointed shoes with four-inch Cuban heels, pitch quarters during lunch, comb their hair in duck tails (a style that requires me to sleep with my hair parted the opposite way so that the curls will straighten out by morning), and who generally get in trouble for everything from smoking cigarettes to belching "The Star-Spangled Banner" in back of Spanish class. It is 1964. School has become intolerable.

My father soon comes to the police station. I am released into his custody and we leave the old armory building of massive, buff sandstone, me in a blue corduroy coat that says Haverford Panthers, my father with his walking stick and tweed overcoat, a cream-colored scarf tucked under his chin. He puts his hand lightly behind me and I involuntarily sink back against his open palm, no easy feat going down a flight of steps. I keep expecting him to ask me what happened. Though I know he won't raise his voice, he never does, let alone physically punish me, I anticipate a lecture, as is his custom when I've misbehaved, which to be honest has not happened all that often. An only child, I have learned how to fill my parents' wishes better than my own. They have little reason to find fault with me, so trained am I in the most subtle of ways—a raised eyebrow from my father, a frown from my mother—to find fault with myself first.

"Why don't we walk a little bit, Ephram." We stop at the post office. My father buys a roll of stamps and some airmail envelopes for letters to Holland. We have no relatives over there anymore but he keeps a regular correspondence with friends and some members of the Amsterdam Symphony. Before the war he, too, had studied the clarinet and planned to become a professional musician, a source of conflict with his father who wanted my father to have a career in business like himself. When I was younger I always eagerly awaited the letters from Holland so I could steam off the stamps for my collection.

We sit down on a bench in front of the post office. It is December but the sun is bright enough for us to rest a moment outdoors.

I am prepared to apologize, no longer able to stand my father's silence. At the same time I want to explain that school offers me nothing but hypocrisy, lies, false values and mush-headed teachers who haven't read a book themselves in years, and that I know this frustration has something to do with what I've done. But before I have the chance, he says he wants to tell me something about the war, one subject about which I am intensely interested because I always hope he will speak, as he rarely does, of his own experience.

"You may not know," he says, "that Hitler had several plans for the Jews. The camps came much later, after he had ruled out other possibilities, such as selling Jews to different countries. He also considered sending the Jews to the island of Madagascar. He wanted to permanently exile them there. Not destroy them, just isolate them on a remote island. This was to be his answer to the Jewish question. I have imagined many times what this situation may have been. I see the beaches, I see the shops, I see the clothes my mother and father wear there—light fabrics, colorful, soft cotton, a little lace on holidays. The sea is blue, the houses white. My mother does not like the heat, but my father welcomes it every morning by doing calisthenics on the balcony. They have settled here, done well, as Jews will do most anywhere, even in Nazi Madagascar. But you see how childish this is of me, don't you? That I want there to be a refuge in the midst of such undeniable evil. Perhaps it is why I decided to study history after the war. I have the liberty to make sense of the many possible pasts historians can always imagine—but the duty to choose only one. Sometimes I fail to honor my task because it is too unbearable. I do not think you are in a very happy period of your life now, Ephram. We are perhaps letting you down, your mother and I. I hope, though, that you will see I am far from perfect and struggle to make meaning of things as much as you do. It is my wish only that you will not harm others in the process, nor assault your own dignity. Leave

yourself a small measure of respect in reserve. Always. You see,
even in my worst memories—and I know nothing that can be
worse for a man than to remember his mother and father and
sister while he walks free in the world—even here I have left
myself an escape to Madagascar. So allow yourself the same
opportunity and do not think so poorly of your own promise
that you must succumb to the disgrace of crime. You are bright,
imaginative, resourceful. Surely there is a way out of whatever
hell it is you too experience. I do not doubt that you can do
better than this."

Chastened, I sit in silence with my father while we drive home.
After his intercession, charges will be dropped by the drugstore.
My mother learns nothing of the incident, and I soon separate
from the group of misfits I've joined earlier. I also give up the
clarinet when I discover—as my teacher agrees—that I feel nothing for the instrument.

My college roommate freshman year is named Marshall X.
Tiernan. I have chosen to go to a small liberal arts college in
Ohio that is not too far from Haverford but far enough so I
feel I'm leaving home. Every Tuesday afternoon he asks if I can
vacate the room for three hours and fifteen minutes (exactly)
so he can listen to music.

"I don't mind if you listen while I'm here," I tell him.

He shakes his head. He must have privacy. Marshall X. Tiernan, reedy and tall as elephant grass but not nearly so uncul-
tivated, has an enormous collection of classical records that takes
up one quarter of our room. He is studying to be an engineer.
Unlike the rest of the men in my dorm, who in the fall of 1968
have grown their hair long and wear patched jeans and army
surplus coats, Marshall dresses in Arrow shirts with button-
down collars and keeps a well-inked pen protector in his pocket.
He has an unfortunate stutter and does not socialize beyond a
fellow engineering student he knows from home. We have a
respectful relationship, but I can't say that Marshall is a friend.

I agree to leave him alone on Tuesday afternoons, but one time I come back early. I have forgotten some notes that I need to take with me to the library. Expecting to hear music outside the door, I hear nothing and decide to go in. On the bed, with large padded earphones, is Marshall, his thin body rigid as slate. He sees me but does not acknowledge that I am here. His clothes, the sheets, everything is drenched with sweat. His legs tremble, a kind of seizure starts. When the record ends, a composition by Satie, Marshall sits up, quickly strips the bed, throws the sheets in the closet (Tuesday the maids bring new linen), changes his clothes and returns to his desk to study.

We do not discuss the incident.

Shortly afterward he drops out of school and moves home. I have the privacy of my own room, a lucky situation that enables me to spend time alone with Jessica, whom I've met at an antiwar meeting. One night while I am telling her, with some amusement I am sorry to say, about Marshall X. Tiernan, I suddenly stop. Jessica says later the look on my face is as if I've seen a ghost, for that is what happens. I suddenly see—no, *feel*—a twenty-one-year-old man curled painfully in a baker's oven, his body kept alive by music.

Thanksgiving vacation my sophomore year I bring Jessica home with me. Several years older than I and a senior in anthropology, she helps my mother with Thanksgiving dinner, talks at length with my father, who retains a lifelong interest in Margaret Mead, and makes such a positive impression on them both that my mother whispers to me as we are about to leave for the airport, "*She's a jewel.*"

But at school I sink into a profound depression. My grades plummet and although Jessica tries to stand by me, I manage to chase even her away. She finds her own apartment yet continues to call every day to check up on me. I become more withdrawn, however, and after a while I ask her to stop phoning. I watch television and eat chocolate donuts, drink milk from the carton and stare at the dark smudge marks my lips leave on the spout.

My father appears one afternoon, a surprise visit, he says. I know by the look on his face, though, that he has come because of Jessica. I burst into tears when I see him.

"What has happened, Ephram?" he says.

But I don't know what has happened, only that I can no longer study, I don't care about school and have no chance of passing finals; I don't care if I flunk out.

"Your mother is very worried. She wanted to come with me but I thought it best if I came alone. Is there anything I can do to help you? Is there something wrong in school, you don't like your courses, the pressure perhaps of too many hours . . . "

"I haven't been to class in weeks," I say. "I can't go. Even a trip to the store is overwhelming." I start to cry again. "I want to go home. I want to go back with you."

"But what will you do back there?" my father says. "There is nothing at home for you now. You have your studies here, your friends."

I look at my father. As always, he is dressed neatly, and warmly, a blue blazer and gray slacks, a wool vest under his coat. Meanwhile, my apartment remains a mess, dishes in the sink, clothes everywhere, my hair unwashed.

"I'll find a job, I'll work and make money."

"And live at home?"

"Yes, what's wrong with that?"

My father pauses. "I don't know. I would think that you'd enjoy the freedom of living on your own."

"I have freedom and privacy at home. You've never told me what to do or when to come in. I'm not happy here."

"But Ephram, changing the place you live will not solve your problems. You need to get to the bottom of this."

"I don't care, I just want to go home! Can't you understand that?" I am almost screaming. "I have to go back. I can't make it here!"

For the rest of the winter I work in a bubble gum factory near Philadelphia. It is miserable, but the more miserable the better because I feel as if I deserve the punishment of tedious, demeaning work for failing in school. I am paid minimum wage, $1.85 an hour. So much sugar hangs in the air—we throw bags of it into a mixing contraption resembling the gigantic maw of a steam shovel—that the people who have worked for years at the factory have lost many of their teeth. The gum itself comes out on long (and unsanitary) splintered boards that I carry to racks, which are taken to another station where these long tubular strips of bubble gum—more like waxy pink sausages than gum at this stage—are cut into bite-size pieces with a tool akin to a large pizza wheel.

One day at the beginning of spring I receive a letter from the draft boad. According to their records my student deferment has expired; I am now eligible to be considered for military service.

My father comes home early from his office hour at school. He himself hates the war, the senseless bombing and killing. He has marched with his college's students and protested the presence on campus of recruiters from a chemical company that makes napalm. He has, in fact, been more active than myself who has withdrawn into the routine and oblivion of factory labor, for which there are no deferments.

"What are your plans?" my father asks.

"I don't know. Canada, I suppose, if all else fails."

"And what is 'all else'?"

"A medical deferment."

"On what basis?"

"My mental condition."

"But you have never been to a psychiatrist. You have no history."

"I don't know then." I shrug. I feel numb, resigned. Why not basic training and then the jungles of Southeast Asia? Could it be much worse than the bubble gum factory?

"You will not go. That is all there is to it. We will make sure of that."

"And how will you do that?"

"We'll hide you, if necessary."

I look at my father and almost laugh. But I can see he is serious, alarmed.

"What are you talking about—hide me? Where?"

He picks up his newspaper and folds it back, once, twice, three times until he has a long strip of news in front of him. It is the idiosyncratic way he likes to read the paper—folding it up like a map until he is down to a small, tight square of information the size of a wallet or obituary. I think that it must make him feel some control over the world's chaotic events to read about them in such miniature, compressed spaces.

My mother brings in a stuck jar for one of us to loosen, and my father puts down his newspaper, which pops open on his lap like an accordion. I am still thinking about his wanting to hide me, aware that the draft has touched off buried fears for him, a flashback to the war, some instinctive response to the personal terror of his family being taken away from him. "I'll get out of it, Dad," I say. "Don't worry. I won't go."

"Don't worry, don't worry, is that what you think is the problem here? You have put yourself in this position, though I begged you not to. What is there to do now but worry!" He stands up. "I am *sick* with worry, if you must know. This is my fault. I should have demanded you stay in school, not let you come here!"

I have never heard him raise his voice like this. His body begins to tremble, and from the kitchen my mother hurries in with her hand over her heart. "What is going on here?" she says. "What are you arguing about?"

"Nothing," my father answers. "The argument is finished," and he goes into his study and closes the door—a sight I am used to from childhood. I hear him weep, but rather than sadness I feel a great relief; finally, something I've done has touched him.

I do not get drafted but receive a high number in the first lottery. The long and tiresome depression, the deadness I have felt, is replaced with the exhilaration of a survivor, a life reclaimed. I make plans to visit Europe, use the money I've saved from the bubble gum factory to travel for three months. Guide-books about England, France, Spain, and Italy cover my bed. I pore over them and come up with a tentative itinerary. But when I actually get to Europe, I find I make a detour from England to Holland. I locate the Jewish quarter where my father hid during the war, find his school—the Vossius Gymnasium—and then what I've come for: the bakery. It is still there, although the original owners who saved my father have long ago died. I explain to the current owners who I am; they tell me in broken English that yes, they have heard what happened here during the war, they know about my father and the Koops who saved him; the story is legend. "Does the oven still exist by any chance?" I ask.

They take me to the back, outside to a shed. It is here, covered with a tablecloth. I ask them if I can be by myself for a few moments and they say certainly, no one will disturb me.

A squat and solid object, the oven stands only chest high. I pull open the door and look inside. The opening is deeper than it is wide, the height a little less than two feet. I hoist myself up to sit on the edge. Then I swing my legs around and push my body in feet first. My neck is back against the left edge. I cannot go any farther. My shoulder sticks out too much even when I bend my knees into my chest. I do not understand how he did this, but I am determined to fit inside, so I slide out again and try to enter without my shoes and without my jacket. I tuck my legs under and pull my head inside, my back curved tight as an archer's bow. I hook my finger through the match hole and close the door. The stove smells of mildew and carbon; the scaled roughness of the iron ceiling grates against my cheek. It is pitch black except for the match hole through which I can see. I put my eye up to it and watch. Soon I hear footsteps and I feel frightened, but the footsteps recede into the distance and the bakery becomes silent.

Many years later my parents come out to celebrate the occasion of our son's fifth birthday. My father helps Philip build the space station they have brought him. I watch them play together, my father with no awareness of the world around him other than this mission to be his grandson's assistant.

While my mother and Judith, my wife, put Philip to bed, my father and I have coffee on the porch. It is a cool summer night and we are in Boulder, Colorado, where the shimmering night sky looks, to my parents, like a planetarium. Judith works in the university's office of communications, while I teach literature. Like my father, I have become a professor.

"What are you going to do now?" I ask him. He is on transitional retirement, half-time teaching, and is scheduled to leave the college next year. "Will you finally go to Europe?"

"Perhaps," he says, "but your mother's back may not permit it."

I nod. The trip out here has cost her a great deal of pain that she has accepted stoically. If she walks for more than half an hour or sits for that long, the result is the same, inflammation.

"Have you thought of going yourself?" I ask.

"I could not leave your mother for that long. She would not be well enough."

My father sits with the hiking boots he has bought for this trip out west laced tight on his feet. They are spanking new and he has already cleaned them of mud from our climb this afternoon. I take pleasure in seeing him so fond of the mountains, so open to the world out here. "You and I could go," I say. "Together. A nurse could help mother if we went next summer."

"I will give it some thought," my father says, but I can see that the veil has already dropped—the complex configuration of blank terror that can still scare me with its suddenness, the yearning on his face vanished. He has gone to Madagascar.

He empties the coffee he has spilled in the saucer back into his cup. "I have made a mess here," he says, replacing the dry saucer underneath. He stands up. Pulls down the sides of his jacket. Despite the hiking boots, he has dressed for dinner. "Would you like to go for a walk with me, Ephram?"

Yes, I say, and get my coat, eager as always.

*   *   *

Last summer Judith and I took Philip to Europe because I wanted to show him where his grandfather grew up. Though the bakery was no longer there—an insurance office now—I described everything about the original building, and the oven. I held him in my arms while he listened with intelligence and care, and I kissed his long lashes and felt his soft cheek against mine. I wondered what he knew that I would never know about him, what pleased him that could not be spoken. When would he grow past me, leave his fatherland, hack and chop and hew whole forests until he could find one piece of hallowed ground on which to plant the seed of his own self?

One night in our hotel I could not sleep and began to write: "Every son's story about his father is, in a sense, written to save himself from his father. It is told so that he may go free and in the telling the son wants to speak so well that he can give his father the power to save himself from his own father." I wrote this on a note card, put it in an airmail envelope, and planned to send it with its Amsterdam postmark to my father.

The following morning a call from my mother let us know that my father had suffered a stroke. We flew home immediately, and I rushed to see him in the hospital while Judith waited with Philip at the house. My mother was there by his bed. An IV bottle was connected to his wrist. His other arm I saw had purplish bruises from all the injections and from the blood samples taken. The effects of the stroke made him confuse the simplest of objects, or draw on archaic uses—a pen became a plume. A part of his brain had lost the necessary signals for referencing things and faces with words, and now dealt in wild compensatory searches to communicate. When he spoke of Judith he referred to her as my husband, called me "ram" trying to pronounce Ephram, and, saddest of all, could not understand why I had so much trouble understanding him. He had once spoken three languages fluently, and to see him in this state was more of a shock than I could bear. When he fell asleep, I left his room to speak with the doctor, a neurologist who explained to me that a ruptured blood vessel was causing the illogical and distorted speech. Bleeding in the brain. The image for me was vivid, his brain leaking, his skull swelling from the fluid's pressure inside and all one could do was wait.

One day while I sat and read by his bed, he said my name clearly and asked if I could help him get dressed. He had a white shirt and tie in the closet. He spoke with difficulty from the stroke, although his condition had improved and we all believed he would be released soon. I dressed him and because he was cold I put my sweater over his shoulders and tied the arms in front so he looked like a college man again. While he sat up in bed I held onto his hand to steady him, reminded of how we used to waltz together when I was ten. I said something to him that I had carried around with me for a long while, something that had no basis in fact, only in the private burden of a son traversing the globe for a father's loss. "I'm sorry if I've disappointed you," I told him and he answered me in speech slowed by his stroke, "I forget everything, Ephram." I nodded, but then cried later at his funeral because I thought and hoped he had meant to say forgive.

ILLINOIS SHORT FICTION